KALEIDOSCOPE

•

Blanche Marriott

AVALON BOOKS
NEW YORK

PRINTED IN THE UNITED STATES OF AMERICA
ON ACID-FREE PAPER
BY HADDON CRAFTSMEN, BLOOMSBURG, PENNSYLVANIA

To my niece, Christine Gravel, who was the source and inspiration for this book.

To my precious mother, Jeannette Gravel, who is never without a story to tell and has always believed in me.

To my loving husband, Walt, whose unfailing support carried me to the realization of my dream.

To my dedicated critique partners, Pat Piscopio, Gail Eastwood, and Karen Frisch Dennen, who pushed and prodded me all the way. We did it, girls!

Chapter One

"**Y**es, my father's name is on the lease, but *I* make the payments. This is *my* business."

Frustration pulsing at her temples, Janeen Warner gripped the phone tighter. Her business, hmph. For how long? All work and no play had left her with an empty purse and a pocketful of principles. The last thing she wanted was for her father to bail another one of his children out of a sticky situation.

While the unwavering trained voice at the other end of the phone droned on about strict policies and limited extensions, Janeen noticed movement on the stairs outside her little sublevel gift shop. Through the glass door, she saw a long pair of legs clad in black, perfectly pressed trousers making their way down the stairs.

Not the usual browser for an ordinary day on the

Market, she mused, returning her concentration to the problem at hand.

"Miss Warner?" the nasal voice on the phone called.

"Yes. Look, I understand your position, and I hope you can understand mine. I'm a little late with the payment, but I will get it to you very soon. I'm sure I'm not the first tenant in Quincy Market to be late with their rent."

Outside, the man in the black trousers talked to a second man in sunglasses. Although she couldn't see their faces, she noted that both seemed upset. Hands waved, fingers pointed. Strange behavior for people about to enter a gift shop. Finally, the man in sunglasses acquiesced and the first man stepped toward her door.

"All right, Miss Warner, but this extension is only for one week. I have certain procedures I must follow."

Janeen sighed with relief. She'd gained some time, enough hopefully not to drag her father into this. Before she could answer the caller, the door signal buzzed and the tall man entered her shop, tipping his dark head slightly so as not to bump the header.

She lowered her voice and spoke closely into the receiver, away from the newcomer. "I promise you. You'll get your money. Just leave my father out of it."

She hung up the phone with more force than she normally would have displayed in front of a customer, but frustration had gotten the best of her. At the sound, the man turned his head slightly, cocking a thick, dark eyebrow in her direction.

Janeen forced a weary smile. She had to make the most of her business while she still had it. The thought of ending up like her brothers, ever dependent on their father, was never far from her mind, and her best reason for pushing just that little bit harder.

"Good afternoon," she said, hoping she sounded more pleasant than she felt. The phone call combined with the long, slow day in the store left her wanting nothing more than to get home to a nice hot bath.

The impeccably dressed man, scanning a rack of postcards, nodded with a hint of a smile. Her gaze slid down to his white shirt collar, red tie, and long, dark gray overcoat. Very traditional, very proper. Black leather gloves completed the ensemble, which Janeen thought a bit flamboyant for such a beautiful April day, even in Boston.

Gloves. How odd. Suddenly a chill ran down her spine. Remembering the other man, she looked to the door. Dressed in a dark suit, which barely disguised his herculean build, he waited outside. His Secret Service–like sunglasses hid the direction of his gaze.

The chill returned. Shopkeepers in Quincy Market had been warned of increasing thefts with the slow economy. Although these men didn't exactly look like petty thieves, their strange behavior put her on guard, her fatigue forgotten for the moment.

Keeping the man outside within her peripheral vision, she returned her attention to the man inside. He'd begun to walk slowly along the opposite counter, looking at the displays. From the side, she studied the strong bone structure of his face and his perfectly trimmed hair with its neat, short sideburns.

"Is there anything I can help you with?" she asked, a slight crack in her voice.

Again he turned his head in her direction, then back to his browsing. "Umm, I'm looking for a gift for my

. . . fiancée." He had a deep melodious voice that soothed her nerves.

Janeen noted the uncertainty of his last word and felt a strange tightness in her chest, the same feeling she got every time her mother asked when she was going to settle down and have some kids. Resisting that biological clock and sticking to her promise to let it tick until she was successful got harder every day. She hated to admit it, but at twenty-eight, she wasn't any closer to success than she'd been at twenty.

"Is there anything specific you're looking for?"

"No, not really. Do you have any suggestions?"

When he finally looked at her straight on, her breath caught in her throat as she stared into the largest, most intense dark eyes she'd ever seen. The classic bone structure she'd noted earlier was softened by smooth, olive skin, and though his nose was large, it enhanced his good looks rather than detracted from them.

Her eyes returned magnetically to his, but she quickly diverted them to the door, afraid to expose her unsettled feelings. The sentry outside still manned his station.

"I, uh, suppose jewelry is always a safe bet." Although her stumbling words betrayed her, she tried not to look nervous.

"I suppose." He looked down at the glass case. "Can you show me something?"

Picking up her keys, she walked over to the jewelry case and brought out a black velvet tray. "What about a pair of titanium earrings?" Without thinking, she shifted into her sales-pitch mode. "A special chemical process brings out the brilliant pinks, purples, and blues which make them so striking."

He gave the jewelry a quick look and shrugged. "She probably has more earrings than she knows what to do with." He ambled over to the next display, his steps slow, almost timed.

After returning the tray to its bed, Janeen relaxed a little, relinquishing her earlier fear of danger. If he was going to rob her, he would have made his move by now.

So why the gorilla at the door?

The man stopped at a tray of scarves. Janeen admired the straight line of his broad shoulders under his gray coat and imagined a well toned body underneath.

As she followed him, she picked up the trailing scent of a sweet cologne that reminded her of the mint cloves in her mother's garden. No doubt it was expensive, as were his clothes. With his gloved hands clasped behind his back, he bent at the waist to inspect the delicate, colorful accessories.

"Those are hand-painted silk scarves. Does she like scarves?" Doing her best to be helpful, Janeen reasoned that if he had money to spend, her job was to help him spend it.

"I don't know." He moved the cuff of his sleeve aside to peek at his gold watch.

"A scarf adds a dash of elegance to the simplest outfit."

"Knowing me, I'd pick the wrong color," he answered helplessly. Quite a contrast to his strong looks.

"Well, what colors does she usually wear?"

"I'm not sure."

This man is hopeless! He was about to marry a woman he knew nothing about. If he had so little insight into what she might like, maybe Janeen should just push him in the direction of some heavier price tags. He certainly could afford it, or so it appeared, and she couldn't afford *not* to try.

"It sounds like you need something different, something not everyone has."

He faced her, arching a black eyebrow. "Such as?"

Again, she was startled by those dark eyes, so penetrating. This time she also noted a hint of sadness, but it quickly vanished with a blink of his heavy lashes.

Janeen moved to an adjacent display case while sorting through her keys. Out of the corner of her eye, she saw his dark form following her, and she told herself to remain calm. He was a customer. Her job was to make a sale, a sizable one if possible. Unlocking the display door, she removed a stained glass cylinder from a wooden cradle.

"What about a kaleidoscope?"

He drew his thick eyebrows together as though surprised she should suggest such an odd item. Looking down at the device she held out to him, the wave of surprise on his face changed into serious interest as he gingerly took the scope from her.

"Point it toward the light over there and look into the lens," she instructed.

He turned his back to her and lifted the scope to catch the light, then exhaled a soft whistle and an indecipherable exclamation.

Janeen never tired of people's reactions to her pieces of art. They reinforced her desire to design more. She wanted to introduce the whole world to kaleidoscopes. *Her* scopes.

"Turn the chamber slowly and watch the colors change."

"This is fascinating!" he exclaimed, obviously enjoying the visual circus before him. "The colors are brilliant!"

"That one's called 'Fantasia.' It's our biggest seller in the line."

He glanced back at her. "You have a *line* of kaleidoscopes?"

"Yes. They're actually quite popular. Here." She brought out two more scopes. The cool leather of his glove brushed the back of her hand as he reached to take one. The hairs on her forearm stood at attention and a tingling sensation raced up to her shoulder. *There must be a draft in here,* she thought.

"I had no idea kaleidoscopes were so sophisticated. The last time I saw one was when I got one of those little cardboard things in my Christmas stocking as a kid."

Janeen smiled at the comment she'd heard a thousand times. "Kaleidoscopes have always been somewhat sophisticated. Through the ages, they were often the gifts of kings and queens."

He looked into the new scope, totally engrossed in the splendor. Turning the chamber slowly, he murmured low appreciative sounds.

She watched him with undisguised pride. She knew the beautiful colors and shapes he was viewing. She knew every one of her scopes like a mother knows her child. "That one's called 'Mirror Mirror' and the other is 'Seascape.' "

"The names are very appropriate," he remarked as he looked into the lens of the second one.

"I try to keep a theme in mind when naming them."

Lowering the scope, he looked surprised. "You name them?"

"Yes, when I design them." She sighed inwardly. She'd had so little time lately to do the designing she loved most.

The surprise on his face now changed to confusion. "You designed all of these?" He looked into the case that held the twelve kaleidoscopes she'd hoped would launch her career.

"Mm hmm." Janeen fiddled with her keys, embarrassed by his admiring stare. She licked her lips. Was that his cologne she could taste? "Well, all but this one," she said, pointing. "This is a Gravelle, one of my favorite designers. I couldn't resist buying it at a trade show."

"Is that how you mass market them?"

"I wish." She gave a soft laugh. "No, right now I only sell them here. Not that I haven't tried elsewhere. It's just a tough market to break into."

"Well, I'm impressed." He smiled, motioning toward the display case. "May I see the rest?"

"Sure." She eagerly brought out the other scopes, confident she had hooked him. A big sale would come in handy right now, especially after that phone call.

She patiently watched as he removed his gloves to better handle the instruments. His fingers were long, slender, and noticeably smooth—not the hands of a laborer. Maybe he was a high finance tycoon, the kind who had regular manicures and used his hands only to sign his name.

Yet they were strong hands—his knuckles bulged when he moved his fingers. They were expressive and sensual in the way he caressed each scope as he looked through it. She presumed his hands were his tools, and he needed the gloves for protection.

The door signal buzzed and two plump, silver-haired women came in, immediately followed by the burly guard in sunglasses. Janeen had almost forgotten about him. She looked from the approaching giant to the unsuspecting ladies, unsure where to direct her attention.

"Go ahead, take care of them," the man with the scopes told her. "I'll just look through these while I wait."

Georgios Andros watched the lovely shopkeeper walk away. She had a classic kind of beauty: creamy complexion, long, dark, silky hair, striking blue eyes, and an extremely curvaceous figure that set his pulse racing. Her navy blue wool skirt hugged her hips gently before it flared around her shapely knees. The white silk blouse flowed over hidden curves with its high cowl neck adorned by a simple gold chain.

But looks weren't what excited him the most. As his manager said, he could get all the beautiful women he wanted without even batting an eye. What truly moved him was the beauty of the creations this woman had designed out of bits of wood, glass, mirrors, and crystals. Creativity and intelligence stirred him more than anything else.

While Tony stood behind him, he continued to inspect the kaleidoscopes at the counter. Their beautiful images inspired music in his mind, music he hadn't heard in a long time, music he'd thought he might never hear again, melodies that had been with him for as long as he could remember.

"Sir?" Tony asked in a low voice.

Georgios chose not to answer. He knew he was stalling, but the trip was inevitable. As soon as he got back in the car, he'd be whisked to Logan Airport for the dreaded recording session in New York. His detailed arguments against it had raised his manager's attention, but in the end made no difference. He had a date with a microphone, ready or not.

Between viewing each kaleidoscope, Georgios stole glances at the saleswoman as she tended to the older women. She dealt with her customers efficiently, taking great care to see that they understood each product. He liked her professionalism. He liked her self-assuredness.

"Sir?" If nothing else, Tony was persistent.

"I know, Tony. I'll be there in a minute. Why don't you wait in the car with Gerald?" He leaned on the glass case and watched the lovely woman at the front of the store as she rang up the ladies' purchases. Her suspicious eyes followed Tony as he resumed his post outside the door rather than in the limo. When she returned to Georgios he couldn't help a broad smile.

"So, do you think she would like one of these?" she asked.

"Who?"

"Your fiancée. Isn't that who you're buying a gift for?"

"Oh, yes." *Get that stupid look off your face, Georgios.* "I wouldn't know which one to choose, though."

He thought he saw disappointment on her face. After all, she was trying to make a sale, and from what he'd overheard of her phone conversation, a good-sized sale was what she needed.

"Do you think she'd like the 'Aristocrat'?" she asked.

He leaned his elbows on the counter, leveling his eyes with hers. "Don't get me wrong. They're all wonderful, but I think I'd like something really special, a one-of-a-kind."

She blinked rapidly. He saw tiny brown flecks in the blue of her eyes, lending them warmth and openness. He felt himself inching forward to see further into their depths, which reminded him of the deep complexities and colors of the kaleidoscopes.

Unmoving and patient, she said, "We have many one-of-a-kind items. Could you be a little more specific?" Her gaze darted to the door for a split second.

Georgios liked this all-business lady. A refreshing change to the falling-all-over-him women he usually had to fend off. The seed of an idea began forming, a plan that would allow him to see her again, and often.

"Do you do custom orders?"

"Uh, of course." She moved back a step, breaking his intentional stare.

He leaned closer and said in a deep, even tone, "I'd like you to make one for me."

"A kaleidoscope?" she asked, unsure of his meaning.

"Yes, I'd like you to design one for me."

"You mean for your fiancée."

"Yes . . . that's right." Catching a glimpse of Tony pacing in front of the door, Georgios straightened up. He towered over the woman who appeared not to believe him.

He looked at his watch again. *Another five minutes and Tony will have my head.* "When do you think you can have it ready?"

She thought a moment. "It's hard to say. I'll need some details about size, colors, shapes. Could you tell me a little about your fiancée so I know the person I'm designing for?"

He liked the way her eyelashes fluttered nervously when she spoke. An image of those soft lashes brushing against his cheeks told him it was time to go.

He cleared his throat. "I'm afraid I don't have time right now, I have a plane to catch. I'll just have to trust your judgment to design something meaningful and . . . unique." He sounded like his manager, telling someone how to be creative.

Georgios reached into his breast pocket for his checkbook and pen. "When is Mother's Day?"

She frowned. "The second Sunday in May, I think."

"I'll need it by then."

The woman's face paled, no longer the blushing rose it had been when she'd talked fondly about her kaleidoscopes. He bent to check the prices of the kaleidoscopes in the display case. Not that he cared about the cost, but if he was to make an impression, he had to do it right.

"That's only four weeks away! It could take that long just to produce it, never mind design it and get your approval." She nervously wrung her hands.

"Like I said, I trust your judgment. Just follow your creative whim." He opened the checkbook and twisted the pen barrel. "I'll leave you a deposit to cover materials and incidentals. Who should I make it out to?"

When she didn't respond, he looked up to see her worried expression. What was wrong? Had she lied? Did she in fact have nothing to do with designing the scopes?

No. He didn't believe that. She'd been too sincere, too proud. Four weeks sounded like plenty of time to him. He'd done his second CD in less time than that. He'd just have to sweeten the pot. Experience had taught him that people do amazing things for the right price and she was apparently in no position to turn down money.

Looking around, he noticed a stack of blue business cards to the right with bold, black script. "Chatter Box?"

She blinked a few times, as though trying to shake the daze and her frozen expression. "I'm sorry, what?"

"Chatter Box. Is that what I make the check out to, the store? Or is it . . ." He looked closer at the business card. "Janeen Warner?" She blushed at the sound of her name. The color turned her radiant under the fluorescent lights.

"Chatter Box will be fine," she answered, distracted.

"And how much do you require?" he asked as he wrote. When again she didn't answer he looked up, tipping his head with anticipation. Janeen squinted; painful indecision seemed to play over her features.

"Maybe we shouldn't bother with a deposit. I'm just not sure I can meet your time frame," she said apologetically.

Ignoring her apprehension, he asked, "Is three hundred enough?"

Resigned to defeat, she sighed, "Yes, that will be fine."

"Five hundred?" He amused himself by bargaining up.

"Three hundred is fine, really." Her face softened.

Georgios searched her eyes for the look that assured him his offer was more than satisfactory. The kind of look he got when he tipped a waitress or a porter a hundred dollars. When Janeen gave him a small, tentative smile, he filled in the check and signed it with a flourish. Quickly tearing it off, he pulled out a business card and dropped both on the counter.

"I'll be out of town for a few days. Just leave a message on my machine when you have something for me to look at."

He lifted her card and held it up to his forehead as though doffing his hat. "Thank you, Ms. Warner. You have been a great help. I hope to hear from you soon."

He hurried out the door to an anxiously awaiting Tony.

Janeen stood transfixed for a moment. So much had happened so quickly, her head felt like it had been in a wind tunnel. The current of air that sailed in the door as he exited served to stir up the scent of his lingering cologne. Out of the corner of her eye, she glimpsed something dark on the counter.

His gloves!

She scooped up the leather accessories and rushed out the door, up the cement steps. Clinging to the railing at the top, she looked to the right, then left. At the end of the marketplace, amongst the milling shoppers, she saw two dark figures climb into a long black limousine. The waiting driver immediately pulled out into the busy street.

Returning to her store, Janeen plopped the gloves back on the counter, causing the check to blow onto the floor. It punctuated how quickly the one month he'd given her would fly by. With all the extra hours she worked to make up for personnel cutbacks, there was little enough time left for herself, never mind another job. Why had she agreed to take on a three-month project that had to be completed in one?

She stooped to pick up the check. This was why she'd said yes. Money. Everything in her life revolved around it: the rent, the bills, the kaleidoscope designs.

If she truly expected to get her own line off the ground, how could she say no to three hundred—

She was stopped in mid-thought after glancing at the check, her heartbeat quickening as she digested the figure.

"Two thousand dollars!"

Chapter Two

For a full thirty seconds, Janeen stared at the name and the amount of the check. Georgios Andros. A picture of his long, expressive fingers almost caressing his gold-plated pen flashed through her mind. She'd watched the point smooth out thin ribbons of ink, forming numbers and letters. Little had she suspected what those numbers would mean to her.

Who was he? Why would he pay her two thousand dollars before she'd even done anything? She picked up his card with the tiny black piano in the left-hand corner. No address, only his name and phone number with a Boston area code. Why a piano? And why had his burly friend waited outside except when customers were in the store?

Shaking her head, she decided to save those questions for later consideration. What mattered most right now was getting the check to the bank to cover her lease payment.

Janeen quickly wrote out a deposit slip, then gathered up her belongings. Her assistant manager would be here any minute to take over for the evening.

As if on cue, Chris Campbell came rushing through the door, spouting excuses. "Sorry I'm late! There was a major backup on the T and I—" She stopped short at the scope counter on her way to the back room. "Hey, what's all this?"

Janeen hadn't had time to put them away. "Would you mind putting those back? I've got to make this deposit before the bank closes."

"Sure. A good day?"

"No . . . well, sort of. We had mostly browsers all day until about half an hour ago. A man came in and asked me to design a special kaleidoscope for his fiancée."

"Cool! What kind of scope?"

Janeen loved the silly, vibrant art student. "I'm not sure yet. But he left me two thousand dollars."

"Two thousand doesn't sound like much for an original. You should've asked for more." Chris, the outspoken.

"That was just a deposit. I have a feeling he doesn't care what the final cost is."

"Super! We could use more customers like that."

Chris started picking up the kaleidoscopes when she noticed the business card on the counter. In a slow, subdued voice, she asked, "Where did this come from?" She held the card with two trembling hands and gazed at Janeen, wide-eyed.

"That's his card. Oh, and those are his gloves." Ja-

neen nodded, indicating the leather pair on the counter.
"You better give them to me before I forget—"

"He was *here? The* Georgios Andros was *here,* in
this store?" Chris's mouth was agape.

"What do you mean, *the* Georgios Andros? Who is
he?"

Chris clicked her tongue and rolled her eyes. "First,
tell me what he looked like."

"He was about early to mid-thirties, dark hair, very
tall, somewhat large nose, nice-looking."

"Did he have the most intense dark eyes?" Chris
crooned.

Janeen shifted uneasily, recalling her own reaction
to the handsome man. But she had to remain professional about this job, especially in front of her employee. "Yes. He did have very piercing eyes," she
answered nonchalantly.

"Oh my God! It was him!" Chris clapped her hands
to the sides of her head. "Why do I miss all the good
stuff?"

"Chris, who is he?" Janeen asked, curious as to how
her young, flighty assistant might know this dashing,
polished man.

"He's a composer. He does contemporary instrumental stuff, what I like to call modern classical music."

"I wouldn't think you'd be interested in that kind
of music." Janeen laughed to herself. Chris personified
the typical art school student, with her colorful, multi-
design outfits and quirky hairdos that changed every
week. Yet they were a part of her open personality,
and customers loved her bubbly disposition.

"Sure, I like all kinds of stuff. I have one of his
tapes and I love listening to it when I'm working in

the studio at school. There's so much emotion in his music. He's a genius!"

"Well, he may be a musical genius, but he doesn't know much about women."

"Why, what happened?"

"I asked him questions about his fiancée, since that's who the scope is for. He acted like he hardly knew her, or cared."

Chris arched an interested eyebrow. In a seductive tone, she suggested, "We-ell, maybe he needs someone more exciting in his life." She fluffed her curly, shoulder-length hair and drew a deep breath into her petite frame. "When is he coming back?"

"I have to call him when I have some designs ready."

"Cool!" Chris lifted the card to study it again. "We even have his home phone number!"

Janeen snatched it from her. "No, *I* have his home phone number, and as a client his right to privacy will be honored."

"Killjoy." Chris appeared wounded, then brightened. "Ooh, wait! I think I have the tape in my carryall." She bent over her canvas tote, never far from her side, pulling out books, notepads, a brush, an empty juice bottle. "Here!" She handed the tape to Janeen. "Couldn't you just melt in his eyes?"

Janeen shivered at the dark penetrating stare from the cover photo. She'd never forget those eyes, but melt? No. She couldn't afford to melt for anyone right now. Her livelihood was at stake. She needed to keep her wits about her.

"Yes, he's very handsome. Now I really have to get going." She picked up her coat and leather bag.

"Here, take this with you." Chris shoved the tape into Janeen's hand.

"What for?"

"Listen to it. You'll love it."

Janeen tried handing it back. "Chris, I'm not really into that kind of music."

"Take it," Chris insisted, "and just listen to it."

There was no time to argue. She had less than fifteen minutes to get to State Street. She dropped the tape in her bag and turned toward the door. "Put his gloves under the counter," she called over her shoulder before the door closed behind her.

Planes had become a second home to Georgios Andros lately. On his way to New York, again, he knew the trip would be just as fruitless as the last three over the past six months. His manager, Michael Conway, wanted to try another session in the recording studio, certain that the magic would happen if he just got Georgios in the soundproof room.

But Georgios knew better. The past year had been a string of silent notes and blank scores. He'd spent many sleepless nights pounding at the keyboard, listening for that perfect melody, that right combination of notes.

It never came. Every composition sounded odd, every arrangement empty. Where had the music he loved so much gone?

He turned to the darkened window of the plane and the diminishing lights of Boston below. The city looked alive, thriving with spirit and originality. Why couldn't he feel that way? Even his riches and fame couldn't buy him an original musical spark. What was wrong?

"Tony, what would you say if I said I was quitting?"

The ever-present bodyguard looked up from his detective magazine. From his seat across the aisle, he stared hard for a moment, then nodded. "I'd say, whatever pleases you, sir." He casually turned back to his reading.

"I mean it, Tony. I'm tired of all this running around. For what? I have no life, no love. I have a million adoring fans, but not one of them knows *me,* the real me. The only life I've ever known is working at the piano for hours on end."

Apparently realizing this was more serious than he'd first thought, Tony put down his magazine and turned in his seat.

"Why don't you take a long vacation? Go to Greece, visit family. Treat yourself to some time off."

"I don't want time off. I want change. I'm tired of trying to create something out of nothing. I used to feel the music all the time, twenty-four hours a day. Now, the feeling is gone. I'm afraid if I don't do something soon, I'll lose myself too."

Tony shifted uncomfortably while his employer bared his soul. The quiet man usually spoke only when spoken to and certainly never about deep personal thoughts. Georgios's manager had hired him as much to guard him as to keep Georgios out of trouble now that he'd achieved superstardom.

"I'm sure if you talk to Mr. Conway, sir, he'll arrange for an extended change of scenery until you get back on track."

"I'm afraid when I talk to Michael Conway you may have to earn your money and protect me."

"Sir?"

"I'm not staying for the recording session."

Tony blinked, then turned back to his magazine. Georgios realized the futility of talking to his bodyguard about a change in lifestyle. He of all people wouldn't want to see the famous Georgios Andros drop out of the limelight. This was his job.

Georgios glanced at his watch and stretched his long legs in front of him, wincing at the limited space even in first class. His gaze returned to the glittering view outside the window. As he stared, unblinking and deep in thought, the lights began to merge and jump. The longer he stared without focusing, the more they moved into geometric shapes and patterns. *Like a kaleidoscope.*

Janeen Warner and her kaleidoscopes had been an unexpected, pleasant diversion that afternoon. After visiting his mother at her elite Greek restaurant, he'd had time to kill before going to the airport, and decided to shop for a Mother's Day gift. The holiday was still weeks away, but he had no idea if he'd have any free time after this trip.

Why he'd told Janeen Warner he was shopping for his fiancée, he didn't know. He supposed it was his manager's warnings to keep his distance from the public. Never let them into your private life. Make one up if necessary.

He'd seen the sign, "Chatter Box," and thought it appropriate for a man of few words. He did his best talking with his music.

At least that's how it used to be. Four CDs in five years, then two years of silence. He'd poured out his heart and soul to the world and suddenly felt completely spent; there was nothing left to say.

Janeen's beautiful kaleidoscopes vividly reminded

him of his dormant creativity, like knocks on closed doors. He thought he'd heard music as he looked through the lenses, and he felt a closeness to the person who created them, as though he'd peered into her soul and glimpsed what drove her.

"Tony," he called across the aisle.

"Yes, sir?"

"Did you tell Gerald to drive right back to that store?"

"Yes, sir. I gave him the five hundred dollars with your specific instructions to spend it on anything he liked, not one penny less. When we land, should I call and see what he bought?"

"No. I don't care what he bought. As long as he spent the money. All of it." He knew Janeen needed the money.

Out of the corner of his eye, Georgios caught Tony shaking his head. What he wouldn't give to know what went through Tony's mind. Five years was a long time to know someone and yet not really know them at all.

Georgios rested his head against the back of the seat. It would be different with Janeen Warner. He would find out everything there was to know about her, what made her tick, what pushed her buttons. He sighed and recalled how her hips had swayed beneath her wool skirt as she moved about the store.

"A penny for your happy thoughts?" The stewardess came by with an assortment of pastries.

"I beg your pardon?"

"You were smiling to yourself. You must have been having some nice thoughts."

"Yes, I was." He continued to smile.

Very nice thoughts, indeed.

* * *

The next day, traffic in the store was a little steadier. Fridays tended to bring out shoppers, spenders in particular, which always brought a sigh of relief to Janeen.

Thinking of spenders reminded her of Georgios Andros and the tape sitting in her bag. She popped it into the system player and listened with one ear as she waited on customers. Several commented on the music. One even recognized it.

"Oh! Georgios Andros. He's wonderful. Boston's favorite son, you know." No, she didn't. She didn't know him at all.

By late afternoon, Janeen waited anxiously for Chris to arrive. Watching the clock, she prepared the bank deposit, then slipped Georgios's tape into her bag. She'd listen to it more closely tonight.

No sooner had she put the tape away than she looked up to see the tall figure in the long gray coat enter the shop, once again leaving his sentry at the door.

"Hello." He smiled, white teeth flashing against dark skin.

"Back so soon? I thought you were going out of town for a few days."

He stopped at the counter directly in front of her, placing his hands atop the glass enclosure. "Yes, well, something came up and my business has been postponed until Monday."

She studied his bare hands—strong fingers, long and lean. "You left your gloves yesterday." She reached under the counter for them. "Luckily the weather has been mild." She placed them on the counter but he didn't pick them up.

"Yes, lucky." He stared with a knowing hint of a smile.

"Is there something I can do for you?"

His smile widened. "As a matter of fact, I've been thinking about your kaleidoscopes."

"Oh, good. Maybe you can give me some insight as to what kind of design you would like. I'd like to do some work on it this weekend."

"As I said, use your own judgment. I'd like something straight from your creative genius."

She laughed. "Creative I can do. Genius I'm not so sure about. With a little help from you, I can try to achieve something personal for her."

"Her?" he asked, almost puzzled.

"Your fiancée."

"Of course." He cleared his throat. "Yes, about that—"

Just then, Chris stumbled through the door, balancing a cardboard tray with a soft drink and sandwich as she looked behind her. "Hey, what's with the guy at the door?"

Janeen indicated with her eyes in Georgios's direction. Chris's mouth dropped to the floor.

"Oh my God!"

"Chris, this is Georgios Andros. Mr. Andros, this is Chris Campbell, my associate. She happens to be a big fan of yours."

"It's a pleasure to meet you, Ms. Campbell." Georgios approached and put out his hand.

"Oh my God!" She gasped again.

"Chris is a student at Massachusetts College of Art. She likes to listen to your music when she's working in the studio." Janeen's awkward explanation did little to shake Chris out of her starstruck spell.

"Why, thank you. It's nice to hear from dedicated fans."

"Oh my God!" Chris whispered, her eyes fixed on Georgios.

"Chris!" Janeen hissed.

The girl turned her curly-haired head and read Janeen's look. "Oh! I'm sorry. I've just never met a celebrity as big as you before," she said to Georgios. "I mean famous! I didn't mean big in the sense that you're tall. Though you are very tall. How tall are you?" She drew her eyebrows together as she looked way up from her mere five-foot-two height.

"Six-two," he answered smiling, obviously amused.

"Wow."

Janeen shifted uncomfortably, bewildered by Georgios's effect on Chris. "Yes, well, I'd like to stick around to hear what else inquiring minds want to know, but I have to get to the bank. Perhaps, Mr. Andros, we could talk some other time." She gathered her coat and bag.

"Can I give you a lift? We could talk on the way."

"Um, I was planning to walk. It's only a few blocks."

"Then do you mind if I join you?"

Her instincts told her no, but her curiosity said, why not? She glanced at Chris, still slack-jawed and of little use.

"Sure, why not."

He looked outside for a brief moment before turning to Chris. "It was very nice meeting you, Ms. Campbell."

Chris nodded, her bouncy curls bobbing in excitement.

* * *

Janeen tromped up the stairs ahead of Georgios, who stopped only long enough to whisper his change of plans to Tony.

"Walk? Sir, I wish you wouldn't. Let me signal the car."

"Tony, I'll be fine. It's just a short walk." He sped off to catch up with Janeen on the cobblestone street. "Hey, you move at a pretty good clip."

"I'm usually in a hurry to get to the bank."

"To deposit all your millions, huh?"

She stopped at the crossing and pinned him with a hard glare. "Far from it."

Ouch. With that icy stare, he knew he'd picked the wrong topic to joke about. "So, what do you do for excitement? I mean other than work, design kaleidoscopes, and go to the bank."

With a tilt of her head, she narrowed her eyes thoughtfully before answering. "Mr. Andros—"

"Please, call me Georgios." A passerby paused with a curious look.

"Fine. Georgios, I don't do excitement. I work, I design, and I go to the bank, sometimes. That's it. That's my life. Now if you're looking—"

"Mr. Andros?" A meek voice from beside Janeen interrupted her awkward comeback. "I can't believe it's you. Could I have your autograph?" An envelope and pen were shoved under Georgios's nose.

He quickly dashed off his signature, smiled, and turned back to Janeen just as the crossing lights changed. They briskly proceeded to the other side.

"Sorry about that. You were saying?"

"Nothing. Let's stick to business. Tell me about

your fiancée. I need something to help me design the scope. What does she like, dislike? Any favorite colors? Does she have a particular hobby or interest?"

"No, you see—" Two women threw their hands up directly in front of him.

"Georgios Andros! Oh my God, it's really you. Would you mind signing autographs for us? We just love your music."

"Thank you. You're very kind." He took the paper offered by one of the women and looked up to see Janeen edging away. He'd just finished signing one and was about to start the other when another woman and her husband stopped. Before he'd finished the second autograph, a small crowd had gathered, and pens and paper came at him from every direction.

His eyes searched the crowd but Janeen had evaporated like mist. He signed each paper with strained enthusiasm and made his way through the crowd as Tony rescued him by signaling to Gerald in the waiting limo.

By the time Janeen left the bank Georgios was long gone along with the hungry fans. She half chuckled to herself thinking about strangers who thought nothing of snatching a moment of someone else's glory. Just what was it about his music that drew them in?

Chris said she had *one* of his tapes, so there must be others. Making a slight detour, Janeen walked to a music store across the Market. Inside, she studied the displays a moment, not sure which section to look in. She didn't have to look far. Atop one of the displays was a large glossy of Georgios Andros, those intense eyes staring at her, warming her cheeks till they burned.

"Do you like Georgios?" Janeen whirled around at the personal question from the salesman behind her.

Her cheeks now flaming with embarrassment, she stuttered, "I . . . I beg your pardon?"

"Georgios Andros. Isn't that who you were looking at?"

Trying to compose herself, she replied, "Y-yes."

"Would you like to listen to one of his selections?"

"No, thank you. I've heard his tape."

"Oh, which one?" The man reached into the rack and pulled out three CDs. "We have three of his last four."

"Yes, that's the one I've heard," she said pointing to *Intimately Yours.* She then took the next one from him, *The Power of Passion,* and stared at the cover. Georgios faced away from the camera, his eyes focused upward, his profile strong. But there was a sadness in his expression, something that made her want to take him in her arms.

"I'll take them all," she said, anxious to get away.

Weary from the long day and the monotonous train ride home, Janeen ached for a hot bath. She felt edgy and restless, but more important, she wanted to learn more about this man who stopped people in their tracks in Quincy Market. Apparently well-known to everyone else, he remained a mystery to her. If she was to do work for him, she needed to know him a little better.

She quickly heated leftover baked macaroni and cheese, and threw together a simple salad. Taking one of the new CDs from her bag, she once again stared at the captivating dark eyes with this strange feeling that she already knew him. She crossed to the living room and slipped the CD into the player.

"Let's see what all the fuss is about."

Settling on a stool at her narrow snack counter, Janeen picked at the crusty edges of the macaroni and cheese. Musical notes began to slowly drift past her; no invasion of sound, just soft music working its way into her senses. Violins and bass drums mixed smoothly to the accompaniment of a piano.

She pictured Georgios sitting at a magnificent piano, his long legs stretched to the pedals, his dancing fingers bringing the ivory keys to life.

The tempo picked up. Janeen caught herself scooping and lifting her macaroni in time with the beat. Her head bobbed with the building crescendo while her foot tapped the rungs of the stool. She felt the music seeping into every fiber of her being, warming her. Never had music affected her like this. Never had she heard anything so beautiful. With closed eyes, she shared the depth of emotion the writer must have felt.

Before the next song began, she hopped off the stool and turned up the volume. For the next half hour, she sat in front of the stereo, immersed in the most magical sounds she'd ever heard, as though the songs were being played just for her. She sensed this composer knew her, knew what would touch her. And she felt that she knew him. He was warm, passionate, creative.

Her mind whirled, images flew at her. Hastily she started the CD again and sat at her drafting table. Picking up her pencils, she listened intently, letting the images chart their own course. Her hand moved as though directly connected to the creative part of her brain. She saw prisms and geometric forms and automatically transferred them to the paper. With colored pencils, she stroked and filled in a full spectrum of beauty.

As each design was completed, she tore the page from the drafting table and let it fall to the floor beside her, finishing the final one just as the last note resounded and the CD went still. Janeen leaned back to inspect the work before her and listened to the silence.

She had no idea how many moments had passed. Gradually, she became aware of sirens crying in the street below her second-floor window. Yes, there was a world out there, but she'd just discovered a new world inside. His world.

The sirens faded to their distant, urgent call. She got up from the drafting table and spread the five sketches on the floor. Tears stung her eyes as she recognized the vibrant feelings she'd captured in her work while listening to Georgios's passion put to music. He'd moved her in a way she never would have imagined possible. Georgios Andros had a power over her. And that frightened her.

By accepting his money she had to fulfill her part of the contract, but could she remain professional? After what she'd just experienced, client or not, she knew she could never look at him again without feeling his music pulsing through her veins, intoxicating her mind. There were two things she had to remember: he was a client, and he was engaged to another woman.

Better she concentrate her energies on her career than on rocking any boats.

Chapter Three

The crowded Market on Saturday afternoon was a good sign for business, but by seven o'clock, the crowds had thinned and Janeen let her two part-timers go. She'd handle the last few hours by herself. She straightened displays, filled out paperwork, and took care of a few customers. But her mind kept returning to the images and sounds of Georgios's music.

She dug *The Power of Passion* out of her bag and studied the photo of the darkly handsome man for some explanation of her distraction. Dressed in a white silk shirt opened at the collar, he stared back sadly. Why so sad? He was rich, famous, and talented. What more could he want?

Slipping the CD into the sound system, she went about setting up the display of her newest oak and walnut chessboard with porcelain pieces. As she laid out the velvet background cloths, the music began to filter through the shop. It soothed and invigorated her at the same time.

She turned up the volume to experience every single note. Gingerly, she placed the chess pieces in a simulated playing pattern. The cool porcelain nearly sizzled against the heat that rose from her skin, heat ignited by the passionate music.

Janeen leaned both elbows on the display stand and let her mind succumb to the building intensity. Like the night before, she saw colors and shapes and movement. Georgios's music stimulated her both creatively and passionately. She was so absorbed in her vivid reflections, she didn't even hear the door signal.

"What's your next move?" Surprised by the deep melodious voice behind her, she turned quickly, knocking over a knight. "I'm sorry," Georgios said. "I didn't realize you were so engrossed in the game." He brushed against her shoulder as he bent to retrieve the white knight that had fallen to the floor.

Speechless, Janeen stared. Was her mind playing tricks on her? Was he really standing there, his long gray coat accenting his towering height? As she took a deep breath, she recognized the cologne he'd worn the day before and knew he was real.

"No, I was just setting up the pieces for a display."

"I'm afraid I've ruined one," he said, rubbing his thumb on the horse's chipped tail, his dark eyes begging forgiveness.

She swallowed hard as her eyes followed the movement of his thumb. "That's okay. A little glue and it'll be good enough for display." She took the damaged piece from him, lingering only long enough to exchange a bit of the warmth of her hand for the cool of his fingertips. It reminded her of his forgotten gloves.

"I have your gloves over here."

"Let me pay for them."

"Your gloves?"

"No." He smiled engagingly. "The chess pieces. The set is damaged."

"Forget it. I told you, I'll use it for display."

He pulled out his wallet. "I insist. It's my fault that one is broken. How much is it?"

"I won't accept your money," she said loudly. Suddenly embarrassed by the loud music—his music—they were trying to talk over, she went to turn down the volume.

Georgios followed her. "I'm flattered," he said, indicating the CD case on the counter.

Fumbling for an explanation, Janeen picked it up. "It's research. I needed to know my subject a little more."

"I would have gladly given you my CDs if I'd known you wanted them." His smile widened.

How different from the somber picture on the case, Janeen thought. She ejected the CD from the player and stuffed it back into her bag. A movement outside the door caught her eye. Once again, Georgios's companion stood by patiently. She bent to shove the bag under the counter and brought out his gloves.

"Here, before I forget."

"Thank you." He held the gloves and lightly slapped the leather against his palm. "I'm sorry about yesterday. I tried to find you after I escaped the crowd, but you'd disappeared."

"It didn't look like you were going to be free any-time soon, so I left before the bank closed."

He nodded. "I came to see if I could make it up to you."

"How did you know I'd be working?"

"I called earlier today."

"Hmmm." She eyed him suspiciously.

"So what would you like to know?"

The closeness of his face as he leaned on the counter sent a flutter through her stomach. "Excuse me?"

"You said you needed to know me a little more. What would you like to know?"

Janeen took a breath, afraid he would hear the pounding of her heart without the music to drown it out.

"I said I needed to know my *subject* a little more— your fiancée. Since you didn't tell me much about her, my only recourse was to learn about you." She re-turned to the chess display to clean up the packaging.

Georgios followed. "And what did you learn?"

Her heart beat so fast, she thought it would stop at any minute. She looked up into his dark, engaging eyes and knew it would be foolish to try to mask her true feelings.

"I learned that you make beautiful music, very mov-ing and inspirational." Her quiet, honest sincerity seemed to surprise him. She had to pull her gaze away to finish her task.

He put down his gloves and reached for her hand as she lifted some tissue paper. She dropped the paper when he brought her fingertips to his warm lips. The kiss was gentle, but long. He seemed reluctant to re-move his mouth from her trembling hand.

"Thank you. That is one of the nicest compliments I have ever received."

Suddenly aware of the futility of surrendering to his flirtations, she pulled her hand back and gathered up the remainder of the wrappings. Isn't that what she'd eventually be if she gave in to his charm? A discarded wrapping?

"Oh, come on. Surely you've heard them all, and your fiancée must swoon over the passionate songs you play for her." Janeen heard the fire in her tone as she said the word fiancée. She quickly retreated to the back room and deposited the refuse.

Georgios met her in the doorway before she came back out. He took both her hands in his, pulling her close. His hot breath blew against her lifted face.

"Do you really find my music passionate?" he whispered.

Her silence answered for her. He lowered his mouth to hers and kissed her hard and hungrily. Frozen by his boldness, Janeen let his lips slide over hers while bass drums pounded in her head. Violins picked up the tempo of blood rushing through her veins. A single, resounding piano played the notes of goose bumps springing up on her skin.

Why was he doing this? Why was she *letting* him do this? Weak all the way down to her knees, Janeen hardly noticed when he lifted his mouth.

With his lips brushing her forehead, he said softly, "I have a confession to make." His hands had slipped around her back and they now massaged little circles against her silk blouse. "I'm not really engaged. I don't even have a girlfriend."

As though shot by a gun, Janeen pulled away from him. It suddenly occurred to her that the rich and famous must get what they want by playing these convenient little games. They say what suits their needs. The adoring public goes along with them because they all want to be a part of the celebrity.

Not this lady! At least not on someone else's coattails.

She brushed past him, back into the store. "I don't believe you. Why would you tell a complete stranger you were looking for a gift for your fiancée if you didn't have one?"

"It was just a reflex, a cover-up," he explained. "I have to fend off a lot of followers in my business."

"I wasn't following you." She stepped behind the cash register, using the counter as a barrier between them.

He sighed in exasperation. "Wait." Georgios went to the door, opened it wide despite the cold night air that rushed in, and asked loudly, "Tony, who am I engaged to?"

The man outside the door looked in at Janeen, then back to Georgios with a very confused look on his face. "No one, sir."

Georgios closed the door again. Janeen crossed her arms in front of her to stave off the coldness that had infiltrated the room. Both men sounded very sincere, but she wasn't ready to give in so easily. "If you have no fiancée, or girlfriend, then who am I making the kaleidoscope for?"

His face turned red and he stuffed his hands into his coat pockets. "My mother," he replied sheepishly.

A laugh escaped Janeen's throat. "Your mother? You expect me to believe that?"

"I told you I needed it by Mother's Day, remember? Every year I try to get her something unusual, something she would never buy herself. I mean, what do you get the woman who has everything? A kaleidoscope is ideal."

He *had* told her the gift was for Mother's Day, even though he'd lied about whom it was for. How much was true and how much was made up to suit his needs?

When she didn't respond, he went to the door again. "Tony, who was I shopping for the other day?"

Again, confused, Tony frowned and looked with disbelief at Georgios. "Your mother, sir."

Georgios closed the door but left his hand on the doorknob. "Any other questions?"

Janeen repressed a smile. "Yes. Who is *he* and why does he stand outside all the time?"

Opening the door, Georgios asked, "Tony, what is your job?"

Now immune to the strange questions, Tony answered matter-of-factly, "I'm your bodyguard, sir." The door closed.

Looking up at the six-foot-plus man before her, Janeen laughed out loud. "You really need a bodyguard?"

"One never knows when I might be accosted by a sexy shopkeeper." He flashed a dizzying smile.

Sexy. That was nice to hear. It'd been a long time since she'd been accused of being sexy. Usually she was determined or businesslike, sometimes even bossy. Sexy had a nice ring to it. She matched the twinkle in his eye with a bright smile.

"So why are you here?"

"To ask you to have dinner with me."

She squinted devilishly at him. "I've already eaten."

His lips formed a half-smile. "Then let's go for dessert."

"I don't close for another hour."

Georgios looked around the empty store. "The place isn't exactly jumping." He reached into his coat for his checkbook. "How much would you normally do in sales for the last hour?"

Janeen's smile vanished. Her eyes hardened. She couldn't believe what she'd heard. "You're not suggesting that you pay me to accompany you, are you?"

"No. I just thought I'd make up for what you wouldn't do in sales if you closed early."

She felt her pulse quicken as her anger rose rapidly. Insulted by his suggestion that it didn't matter how she made her money, she glared at him for a moment before responding.

"Is that what you celebrities do? Buy other people for your own pleasure? If you weren't so shallow and self-absorbed, you'd see that some of us have feelings and principles."

Georgios tucked his checkbook back into his pocket. "You're taking this the wrong way. I just don't want you to lose out."

"On what? Dinner with you? What makes you so sure that I would want to have dinner with you? Just because you're rich and famous doesn't mean everyone is impressed. I'd like to think I have a little more character than that."

"I never questioned your character for a moment." He reached for her hand, but she pulled it away.

"Then why did you want to pay for a chess set that I broke, and why did you insult me by offering to pay for my time?" He opened his mouth, but she hurried on. "I'll tell you why. Because you think you can use your money to buy anything you want. You are the famous Georgios Andros, Boston's favorite son." She held her eyes steady on his. "Well, it won't work here. You and your checkbook can leave now. I have a business to run. And for future reference, I can't be bought."

Chapter Four

"**Y**ou look tired, dear. You must be working too hard." Janeen's mother dumped a pot of steaming potatoes into a large bowl and stood back from the escaping vapors.

Janeen knew where her mother's comments were headed and that there was no stopping her. In a controlled tone, Janeen said, "I have to work hard, Mom. I run a business."

She hated this Sunday dinner ritual, pretending everything was fine in front of her family. But she'd decided a long time ago to keep her problems to herself, unlike her brothers, who recited a litany of woe-is-me complaints.

"But do you have to work so many hours? You're going to run yourself into the ground before you're thirty-five."

Janeen took the masher from her mother and

jammed it into the potatoes. "Dad runs a business and works long hours. I don't see you complaining about that." Unintentional sarcasm had slipped into her tone. She'd been down this road before.

"That's different. He's a man."

Janeen stopped mashing. "Mom, why is it okay for a man to work long hours in a business, but not a woman?"

"I didn't say it was wrong. I just don't think *you* should be doing it." Here it comes, the lopsided logic she'd been spoon-fed since she was old enough to climb trees. "You should be going out, meeting people, finding yourself a husband. They'll all be gone before you get around to looking."

That's it! If she heard one more speech about settling down and having kids. . . .

Janeen tossed the masher into the sink and delivered the bowl to the dining room. With a thud, she plopped it on the table near her brother Robbie. "Here, pass this around."

Through shaggy bangs, Robbie gave her a side-glance. "What's eating you?"

"You wouldn't understand," she grumbled, as she sat down in the empty seat near him.

"Oh, one of those women things, huh?"

She slapped her palm down on the table. "Why is everyone in this family so obsessed with *women* things and *men* things? I feel like I'm back in the caveman days. Any minute now an apeman with a big club will come in and drag me off by my hair."

"Might do you some good," Robbie mumbled.

"Yeah, and it's the only way you'd ever be able to hold *on* to a woman," she snapped back at her divorced brother.

"All right," Mr. Warner interrupted, "it's been a rough week. Let's settle down and have a nice peaceful meal."

She looked around the table at the guarded faces. Her father and mother exchanged a look of helplessness. Robbie concentrated on cutting his roast into bite-size pieces. Tim's wife shot nervous glances from her husband to Robbie.

"What happened? Did I miss something?" Janeen asked.

Tim, her oldest brother, was the only one who looked her in the eye. Robbie continued to shovel food in his mouth and waved a hand at Tim as though signaling to spill the beans.

"Robbie lost his job this week."

The words hung in the air. *Again,* Janeen thought, but she knew she couldn't say that out loud. "Oh. Sorry to hear that, Robbie. I could ask around at some shops in the Market—"

He shook his head and mumbled between mouthfuls, "Nah, I'll work with Dad until something better comes along."

She wanted to slap him. She wanted to call him an ungrateful leech. But one look at the hurt in her father's eyes told her not to make matters worse. Robbie had always treated their father's woodworking business as beneath him.

The dark paneled walls of the small dining room closed in on Janeen. She needed fresh air. Pushing her chair back, she walked out to the back porch and leaned on the railing. Clouds had rolled in off the ocean. Seagulls squawked overhead as if angry that the winds had pushed them so far inland. Even the air seemed unhappy as she inhaled a musty smell.

Her father joined her at the railing, his thin figure barely casting a shadow. "He needs our support right now, not our disapproval."

"He's a spoiled brat who thinks of no one but himself," she snapped. "He thinks he can do whatever he wants and never have to answer for any of it."

"He's had to answer for plenty." Her father's low, sad voice carried the weight of all the troubles he'd faced since Robbie was a teenager.

"No, he hasn't. You've done all the answering for him. He lost another job and came running back to you knowing you'd take him back, again."

"What am I supposed to do? Throw him out on the street?"

Couldn't he see neither of his sons had any backbone and never would develop one if he didn't let them? She heard the pain in his voice, yet she couldn't stop herself from venting her frustration.

"You can't bail him out of every jam for the rest of his life, Dad." Her voice began to quiver. She'd never spoken so boldly to her father, the man she admired more than anyone. "At some point, he has to be accountable for his own actions."

"As long as I am able, I will always do whatever I can for my children. All of them."

"Dad, we're not your responsibility forever. We have our own wings to fly and our own nests to build."

"And sometimes there's just that little extra help you might need. If so, I'm there."

Realizing her scene with Georgios last night had soured her mood, she tried to explain her reasoning to her father.

"Dad, don't get me wrong, but I don't want your help. I want to do things on my own, achieve my own success with my own skills. I guess it's a sense of pride I got from you. I went along with your co-signing the lease agreement because it was the only way I could get the shop. I had no credit history. But I've made every payment on my own and I'm proud of it."

He put a rough hand over hers. "I'm proud of you too."

She shivered. If only he knew how close she'd come to asking him for money for the last lease payment. It would have been her undoing, the end of her staunch principles.

But Georgios Andros had been her savior with his deposit; at the same time bringing a new set of problems into her life.

"By the way, Dad, I might need a favor, a special rush job."

Howard Warner smiled. "Oh! My money isn't good enough, but my woodworking shop is, huh?"

"This is business; I'll pay for your time. I have a client who might need a scope in a few weeks. Can you fit it in?"

"Might? Why doesn't he know if he needs it?"

She couldn't tell him she'd thrown the client out of her shop and he might never come back or speak to her again. On the other hand, she'd taken his down payment, and by rights had to make good on her end of the bargain.

"We haven't worked out the details yet," she explained.

"You just get me the designs, I'll get you the cylinders. As I said, I'm always there for my children." He tugged at her elbow. "Come on, dinner is getting cold."

* * *

"It's not working, Michael!" Georgios shouted through the thick glass. He'd arrived at the recording studio early Monday morning and already felt as though the walls were closing in on him while his manager and technicians stood on the other side calmly smoking their cigarettes.

"Let's give it one more try, Georgios. You just need to loosen up. It's still early." Michael Conway knew how to manage, but he had no idea how to make music.

Georgios shut his eyes, frustrated. He'd wasted his time coming to New York, knowing what the results would be. He wasn't ready to create and no amount of coaxing was going to change that. The question was, would he ever be ready?

Shoving back the piano bench, he headed for the padded door. "I'm as loose as I'm ever going to be," he grumbled as he brushed past the control panel, heading for the exit.

"Wait!" Michael called. "I'll come with you."

"Where? Where are *we* going to go, Michael?" He stood in the doorway, waiting to make his exit. Alone.

"Anywhere you want. Let's get some coffee and talk."

"Talking isn't going to help. That's not what I need."

"Then, what? What is it you need?" Michael's face showed the strain of managing an impossible artist.

But Georgios knew he wasn't impossible. He'd always been a model client, hadn't he? His last four CDs were cut like clockwork, he never complained about his concert schedule, and he went along with all the promotional appearances. What more could a manager want?

An artist who produced.

"I guess I don't know what I need, Michael. But I know it's not here. I told you last Friday I wasn't ready. Why couldn't you believe me?"

Michael jingled the change in his pocket. "I thought it would click once you got here."

"Well, it didn't. And I don't know if it ever will. In fact, I don't know if I want it to." Georgios leaned his arm against the doorjamb.

Michael gasped. "You're not serious, are you?" He stopped jingling his change. "What's happened to you?"

Georgios stared over Michael's shoulder at the geometric pattern of the sound walls. He almost laughed at the irony of the situation. If he stared long enough, the shapes moved, just like the city lights from the plane.

"A kaleidoscope," he murmured.

"What?" Michael's face screwed up in confusion.

"My life is like a kaleidoscope. Everything is all jumbled up inside this long cylinder. Everyone keeps looking in to see what's there, but until I can get it into focus, no one will see anything clearly, including me."

"What are you talking about?"

Georgios rubbed his forehead against his arm. "I'm talking about me. Something inside of me needs change. The music alone just isn't enough. There's a big empty space that needs filling, and if the music can't do it, I have to find out what will."

Michael stood dumbfounded for a few seconds. He

lowered his voice and moved closer. "Can't you just try once more? These guys are being paid for four full hours. Bad enough I had to pay them for Friday when you didn't show up."

Georgios stiffened. Conway hadn't heard a thing he'd said.

"It's my money and I'll spend it or waste it any way I like." He turned and pushed the door open to his freedom.

"Where are you going?" Michael called.

His footsteps clicking a beat down the empty hall, Georgios shouted over his shoulder, "To get my life into focus."

Chapter Five

Janeen faced another workweek wondering how far she could stretch a dollar. With sales down twenty percent, she didn't know how long she could hold on. On the up side, it was Patriot's Day, a holiday unique to Massachusetts, and Boston in particular. The Market promised to be jammed with tourists for the marathon.

Preparing the cash drawer, she noticed Georgios's gloves still on the shelf underneath and felt the hurt of his insult once more. Did he solve all his problems with his checkbook? She wondered, too, if he still expected her to make the scope. What if he asked for the deposit back? The money was long gone and she'd be hard pressed to replace it.

As expected, customers came in droves. By mid-afternoon, Janeen was glad to see Chris arrive early as she'd promised. Two hours passed before the crowds thinned to mainly lookers. Anxious for feedback from Chris's keen artistic eye, Janeen brought out the kaleidoscope sketches.

"What do you think—will Mr. Andros like one of these designs?"

"Janeen, they're beautiful, and you did them so quickly!"

"Yeah, I was feeling creative."

Chris gave her a squinty-eyed look. "I can see he made more of an impression on you than his checkbook did."

Janeen turned her head to hide the redness she felt rising on her neck. "Don't be silly. He's just a client."

"So, there's no law against dating a client."

"Sorry, he's not my type."

"How do you know? Give him a chance."

"Chris, I'm not looking to give anyone a chance right now. I don't have time for romance or one-night flings."

"Well, if you don't want him, can I have him?"

Janeen jokingly shoved Chris in the direction of the door. "Go get us some sandwiches."

Enjoying the momentary quiet, she sat on a stool behind the register, flexing her aching feet. When she saw the long legs coming down the stairs, she held her breath. *It can't be.*

Georgios came in, his face guarded. He wore a short leather jacket, zipped halfway, a white pinstripe shirt, and a red tie. As usual, perfectly attired. He stared a moment, waiting for her reaction. "I believe I left my gloves here, again."

She reached beneath the counter for the gloves, keeping her emotions in check.

"Thank you." He stuffed the gloves into his pockets, then walked over to the chessboard display. "I'd like to buy this chess set."

She hopped off the stool. "I'll get one from the back."

"No. I want this one," he said emphatically.

"You know it has a broken piece," she reminded him.

With a smile, he said, "I have a soft spot for wounded animals. Besides, it has sentimental value."

"And am I to believe you are sentimental, you who acquires and discards fiancées so easily?"

"Ooh, that's hitting below the belt." He faked an injured look. "But deserved, I suppose. I'll forgive you for the comment if you'll forgive me for the unintentional ruse."

"I doubt that a man like you does anything unintentional."

"Are you implying that I'm calculating?"

She tilted her head. "That's one way of putting it."

"What did I do that was calculating?"

"First of all, the two-thousand-dollar deposit."

"I have no concept of money." He jutted his chin out.

"Second, your attempt to retrieve your gloves, which you ended up leaving behind again." She smiled with satisfaction.

"I'm absentminded."

"Third, your ploy to pay me to accompany you."

"Okay, that was a mistake. I'm bad at the dating game." He moved closer. "Anything else?" His eyes blazed with excitement. "What about the kiss? Was that calculating?"

"Very," she stammered.

He bent his head close to hers and whispered, "And what if I did it again? Would that be calculating?"

Her blood raced. He'd wriggled his way onto her good side again with his charm, good looks, and innocent manner. But she wasn't about to give in so easily.

Chris came stumbling through the door, glancing behind at Tony standing guard, sandwiches and drinks tipping in every direction. She placed them on the counter and smiled brightly at Georgios. "Hello again. You're becoming a regular here."

"And you are very observant."

Chris giggled as Georgios blasted his full wattage smile. "And it looks to me like you haven't quite found what you want in the store." She slanted a gaze toward Janeen.

"Chris, why don't you start on your sandwich," Janeen suggested. "I was about to help Mr. Andros with a purchase."

Georgios moved closer to Chris and in a soft tone said, "Actually, maybe *you* can help me."

Chris beamed. "Sure! What are you looking for?"

He bent down, put a conspiratorial arm about her shoulder, and said, "I'm looking for a way to get Ms. Warner to have dinner with me tonight. Can you help me out here?"

Chris's glow dimmed for a moment before she nodded. "Oh, she's not as tough as she acts. If you tell her you're going for Chinese, she'll be like putty in your hands."

"Chris!" Janeen gasped at being sold out so quickly.

"Go on," Chris cajoled. "I'll be fine by myself."

"Sorry," Janeen said, nodding toward her sandwich. "I already have my dinner plans and it may get busy again later."

With a shrug, Chris unwrapped Janeen's sandwich and ceremoniously dropped it on the floor. "Oops! I'm such a klutz. Guess you'll have to make other arrangements for dinner."

Georgios clamped a hand over his mouth, stifling the laughter that shook his shoulders. Janeen looked from one to the other, squinting venomously.

"This is *not* funny," she warned. Then, as Georgios put on a serious expression, Janeen glanced at the ruined sandwich, while her own laughter struggled to the surface. The trio exchanged looks and all burst into laughter at the same time.

With tensions eased, Georgios asked, "Does this mean yes?"

At least he wasn't offering to pay her this time, a marked improvement. Sighing, Janeen replied, "Under one condition."

"Name it."

"You take off your tie." She said it jokingly, but she really wanted to see if he could relax, be an ordinary Joe.

As though not quite comprehending what she'd said, he touched his fingers to his tie and slowly began to work at the knot. Then, with a sudden flourish, he whipped off the silk finery and tossed it to the floor. "Ta da!"

Janeen had never ridden in a limousine. She was amazed at the plush leather and velvet, the phone, the stereo system, the mini-fridge, the countless buttons that connected to who-knows-what. Georgios had more luxury in that vehicle than she had in her entire apartment.

He tapped on the smoked glass separating them from the front seat. Tony slid the window open for his instructions.

"Call Ming," was all Georgios said.

Janeen could see Tony's hulking figure silhouetted against the oncoming headlights. He picked up a phone, then turned to Gerald, the driver, and spoke a few words while signaling some directions with his hands. She shook her head. The employment of these two men was completely dependent upon the success of the tall, dark, handsome man next to her. Such an extravagance.

"Does Tony go everywhere with you?"

"Pretty much." Georgios tilted his head as though he hadn't really thought about it before.

"Why do you need a bodyguard? Have you been threatened?"

He laughed. "No! My manager hired him to protect me from myself, to make sure I don't do anything to hurt myself."

"I see." But she didn't really. She'd lived in the big bad city of Boston for the last four years and had learned how to take care of herself. Why couldn't he? "Don't you sometimes find it annoying to always have him hanging around?"

Georgios turned to her with a concerned look. "Does having Tony around bother you? I can ask him to leave."

"Don't be silly. If his job is to protect you then let him do his job. I was just curious." The last thing she wanted was to see someone else out of a job.

Gerald turned the huge car off the road and slowly pulled up to the entrance of Ming Gardens, a Chinese restaurant she'd heard rave reviews about. While Tony held the door open, Georgios got out and offered his hand to Janeen. She felt as though she should be wearing a ballgown and glass slippers.

Once inside the elegant but simple restaurant, the trio was ushered to a private room with its own little garden and waterfall. Janeen ogled the dainty plants and lush flowers tagged with names she couldn't even pronounce. At the far end of the garden stood a small Buddha-like statue surrounded by ferns and assorted greenery. Simple black shelves with colorful porcelain and pottery from the Ming Dynasty lined the walls.

Georgios held out a black lacquered chair so Janeen could take a seat facing the garden. When he removed his leather jacket, she noticed his well-shaped body. The tailored shirt fit his masculine form like a glove, revealing broad shoulders, a tight chest, and a flat stomach. His black pants, pleated to perfection, hung stylishly from his trim waist.

"Would you like a drink before dinner?" he asked.

"No. If I drink, I'm liable to fall asleep."

"Am I that boring?" He looked offended.

"No, I'm just not much of a drinker."

"Good. Neither am I."

As though some signal had sounded, a waiter and a waitress came in and began serving rolls and tea and delicate vegetables. The countless courses that followed were a welcome distraction to Janeen who knew so little about the man across from her and even less what to talk about. They were worlds apart. What could they possibly have in common?

Janeen drained the last of her tea from the tiny cup

and watched Georgios crack open his fortune cookie. He looked up and gave her a sly smile as he read, "You will meet a beautiful woman who will change your life."

A blush warmed her cheeks as she looked down into her cup.

"Aren't you going to open your cookie?" he asked.

She shook her head. A strand of hair fell over her eyes; she quickly flipped it back into place. "I don't like to tempt fate. I'd rather take it as it comes. Things are bad enough. I don't want to know if they're going to get worse."

"But suppose it's good? Look at mine. I'm going to meet a beautiful woman who will change my life."

"Considering the circles you run in, I'd say it's highly likely."

"Ah, yes. But I met her in a cute little gift shop, unaware of the effect she had on me."

Janeen shifted in her seat. Though her heart pounded and her palms began to sweat, she considered his romantic innuendoes cautiously. She needed to keep her head clear and not allow the glamour to blind her. It would be too easy to let herself be swept off her feet. The hard part was avoiding it.

She looked into Georgios's dark eyes, searching for the depth of his sincerity. "How could I change your life? You're famous, established, rich. Nothing I can do would change that for the better."

"That's where you're wrong."

After a light tap at the door, Tony entered. "Sir?"

"What is it, Tony?"

"Mr. Conway's on the phone. He'd like to speak with you."

"Tell him I'm busy."

"Gerald did, sir, but he insisted that he speak with you."

"Tell him my decision stands. I have nothing more to say."

Tony left. Georgios took a long sip of tea, then stared at the miniature cup as though it held the answer to some secret. He finally put it down and relaxed in his chair with a sigh.

"Now, where were we?"

Janeen wasn't about to remind him he thought she could change his life. She'd be happy if she could change her own!

"Oh, yes. Now what can you do to change my life? How about that kaleidoscope for starters?"

He still wanted to retain her. Thank goodness. "I've done some sketches on a few designs."

"Good! When can I see them?"

"Whenever you'd like. They're in my bag in the car."

Georgios went to the door and summoned Tony. "Please go to the car and get Ms. Warner's bag."

Feeling awkward and not used to being waited on hand and foot, Janeen said, "Maybe this isn't such a good time. There are five designs and the sketches are quite large. There wouldn't be room on this small table."

He turned back toward the door. "Then I'll have another table brought in."

"No!" He had an answer for everything! There were no such things as obstacles. Just give an order, spend some money, and he had anything he wanted.

He stood by the door, puzzled. "You don't want another table?"

"Uh, no." She looked around, groping for an alternative. "The floor! It's clean, the rug is soft. We can spread them out on the floor and you'll get a good bird's-eye view."

"All right."

Tony knocked again and slipped in far enough to hand the bag to Georgios who brought it over to Janeen.

"Are you sure we have time for this?" she asked.

"I have no other plans, do you?"

"I mean the room. Shouldn't we leave now that we've finished our meal?"

"The room is ours to stay as long as we like."

Of course, how silly of her to think otherwise. He'd seen to the arrangements while they were in the limo.

From her bag, she brought out the designs folded in a large suede pouch. One by one, she spread them on the floor using her shoe to straighten a corner here and there.

"As you can see, I've decided that wood will house the unit in each design. My father owns a woodworking shop, so he can make it rather quickly, if I beg a little."

Georgios bent to inspect each sketch. She waited for his comments, but he made none as he went from one to another, squeezing his chin, tapping his lips, nodding in agreement. His silence made her crazy. Did he like them or not?

"They're good. Very good. How did you get so much detail in so many different areas in such a short time?"

"I guess I was inspired." *If he only knew.*

"It shows." He crouched down to get a closer look. "Explain some of the workings to me."

She crouched next to him, glad she had worn her

long red pleated skirt. She went through her descriptions, careful not to let it slip that his music had been the instrument behind her hand. But would he know? She wondered. When she finished her presentation, he took her hand and pulled her up as he rose.

"They're beautiful." He touched her temple with the back of his fingers. She shivered as much from his light touch as from the sincerity of his compliment. "There's a lot of you in these designs, I can see that." His fingers worked their way into her hair, combing back the thick locks that fell forward over her shoulder. "There's a lot of love in that work."

He bent forward and touched his lips to hers. Remembering their kiss in the back room of her shop, she sighed hungrily, moving closer to catch his impending kiss. But he held back, feeling her lips with his own, letting their mouths touch but not press. The light-as-air movement awakened a hundred little sensitive points all along her heated lips.

His other hand slipped about her waist to pull her closer. She wrapped her arms around his back and felt his firm muscles tighten as he stroked her hair again and again.

"You're very talented," he said. "You're not afraid to show yourself in your work. I admire someone who can create tangible works of art from inspiration. I admire determination. So few people are determined enough to carry out their dreams."

He kissed her again, harder this time, with an intensity that belied his usually calm exterior. Janeen responded just as intensely. Her hands held his back tightly. Every part of her body felt warm and alive. Georgios lifted his head and stared hard into her eyes.

"You're so beautiful, so intelligent, so talented.

From the moment I looked into that first kaleidoscope you handed me, I knew I wanted to be with you. I saw things that made music play in my head, as though we were in tune with each other's creativity."

She brought her hand around and rested her palm on his chest. Absently she let her fingers roam along the muscular expanse. Glad that she'd made him remove his tie, she settled her fingers on the thatch of hair exposed by his open collar. With the mixed feeling of roughness and silkiness intoxicating her mind, she forgot her earlier caution.

"It's funny you should say that, because I listened to your CD that night. That was what inspired these sketches."

He nuzzled her ear, breathing warmly against her neck. "I knew it. It wasn't just wishful thinking on my part."

He pulled her tightly into his arms and they kissed for what seemed like hours. As Janeen drank in every ounce of his passion, she wondered about his comment. Did he really know?

After a light knock on the door, Tony entered again. Georgios did not loosen his embrace.

"Sir, Mr. Conway would like to speak to you."

Georgios turned his head sideways, toward Tony. "I told you to tell him I was busy."

"Sir, he said he won't take no for an answer."

Georgios turned sharply and faced Tony. "Tell him there isn't even a question. I'm *not* going back."

Tony left. Janeen watched Georgios's face struggle for composure. She wanted his arms tightly around her again, to see pleasure and adoration in his eyes. But something had intruded on their few moments of intimacy, and it wasn't just Tony.

"Who is Mr. Conway?" she asked.

A small sigh escaped him. "My manager."

"Isn't it usually important when your manager wants to speak to you?"

He gave her a longing gaze. His fingers brushed her temple again with soothing strokes. "Not anymore."

She pulled back from his touch. "Not anymore? What do you mean? Why aren't you going back?"

He smiled and reached for her hands. "I quit. I'm out of the music business." He watched Janeen's face go from shock to disbelief. Her soft hands trembled slightly.

"You're joking, right?" she asked. "You're just playing hard to get with your manager, to make a point."

Since that morning, he hardly believed himself that he'd made such a drastic move. But the minute he'd walked out of that studio and onto the plane, a feeling of well-being had come over him. A tremendous burden was lifted from his shoulders and he felt free, free to do what he wanted. No longer did he need to worry about music, or deadlines, or pleasing the record company. It was about time he thought about what pleased him.

"No," he smiled. "I may play hard to get with groupies or journalists, but never with my manager. And I hope never with you." He touched his lips to the backs of her hands. They were soft and tasted like lemon drops.

She pulled her hands away quickly, moving back a step while crossing her arms in front of her.

"How can you be so calm about this? You've just thrown away a brilliant career as though it were an old pair of shoes." She raised her eyes to the ceiling, as if searching for an answer. "Some of us struggle every day of our lives to attain a level in our career we can be proud of. I could never justify throwing it all away once I'd achieved it. How can you?"

The fire in her eyes revealed a sensitive issue deep within her. He tried to gather her in his arms again, but she would have none of it. She turned her body away from him.

"Let's sit." He offered her his hand, motioning toward the table. She reluctantly accompanied him to their seats. Georgios took a deep breath. He held her gaze steady with his own as he struggled to form some logic out of what appeared totally illogical to everyone else.

"Music has been my whole life—writing and performing. I loved it and it came so easily to me. The success, the money, the acclaim. All I had to do was sit at the piano and the magic happened. I was a golden boy. I was also oblivious to what went on behind the scenes. My managers—I've had three—always took care of schedules, contracts, promotions, and just about anything else in my life. I made the money, they made my life simple." A slight chuckle escaped his throat. "It's amazing how much is done for you when you have money."

In a flash, he remembered the day he was showering and it suddenly occurred to him that he had no idea where the clean towels came from. He never saw anyone bring them in or take the dirty ones away. Everything was done for him.

Janeen's expression softened and she leaned forward, her arms on the table. "Why didn't you just say you were unhappy about the arrangements?"

"But I wasn't. I was happy. All I had to do was write some music and play it to the best of my ability. The managers made the rounds selling it to television for background music on soap operas and sporting events. Once in a while a piece was picked up for a movie or a commercial. My life was on an even keel and royalties floated in. I took my work for granted."

He paused to put his thoughts in order. He'd never really analyzed his life in such detail as he was doing now for Janeen.

"Then about seven years ago we went into the studio for my first CD. It was hard work and completely draining at times, but I felt myself coming to life, no longer dispassionate. My music gave me strength and power—a power of passion."

She smiled a shy but affectionate smile. "The title of your CD."

He reached across the table to cover her hands with his, stroking her soft skin with his thumbs. "As quickly as the passion had come, it disappeared five years later. Live concerts and touring merely had the effect of a temporary injection of adrenaline. Once I got back to just me and the empty score sheet, the energy was gone. It was as though the artistic part of my brain had fallen asleep."

She tilted her head sympathetically. "Maybe you just need a vacation, time away from all the hubbub and pressure."

He shook his head. "I've tried it. It didn't work. No, there's something missing in my life."

He couldn't tell her how instrumental she'd been in helping him make this decision. When he first met her in the gift shop, he'd only meant to spend a little money after catching the gist of her phone call. He'd delighted in the whim and happily paid for an extravagant kaleidoscope.

Now, there was much more at stake. If he had lost his music, he wanted the chance to be like everyone else—to pursue a dream, to love and be loved. And he could think of no better way than to start with the beautiful woman across from him.

Chapter Six

"What about you?" Georgios asked, hoping to take the spotlight off his dilemma. More importantly, he wanted to know about her. Everything. What made her happy, what made her sad, what made her tick. With a squeeze of his hands, he urged, "Tell me about yourself."

Janeen blushed. "I'm just a simple girl with a dream."

"And what is your dream?"

"Certainly nothing as elaborate as what you've known."

He stared deeply into her soft eyes. Surely if he looked deep enough, he would see the depths of her soul.

"Then what motivates you? What makes you do what you do?"

She looked past his shoulder, to the garden and statue. Her clear blue eyes reflected a far-off longing.

"When I graduated from Massachusetts College of Art, I took almost any design job that came along: jewelry, stationery, book covers. It was fun, but nothing was as fulfilling as the months I'd spent working on my degree project—kaleidoscopes."

"So, you've accomplished what you wanted. You have your own shop and your own line of kaleidoscopes." His voice seemed to snap her back from where she'd allowed her thoughts to drift. He almost felt guilty for interrupting her journey.

Sadly, she replied, "No, not quite. The shop is a means to an end. I want to sell my scopes on a large scale in prestigious markets. My dream is to make Janeen Warner synonymous with beautiful kaleidoscopes."

Georgios laughed. "How strange. You're struggling to get into the limelight, and I'm struggling to get out."

Instead of joining his laughter, she gently withdrew her hands. "Talk about opposites, huh?"

She pushed her hair from her strained face. It tore at his heart to see her struggle with something so obviously painful. His pointed questions only served to bring her pain to the forefront. He had to find a way to ease her sorrow.

"Oh, I wouldn't say we were total opposites. We both like my music. We both like your kaleidoscopes." He picked up her discarded fortune cookie. "And we both like Chinese food."

With a sharp twist, he cracked open the cookie and tugged the delicate slip of paper from the crumbled confection. His smile broadened. "It says 'Reach for a star. It will carry you to heaven.' See, it *is* a good fortune."

"Unfortunately it's just words on a piece of paper. Real life is a little more complicated." She rose and began to gather up the sketches from the impromptu floor display.

Georgios went to her side. "Maybe I can help make it a little less complicated."

"Yes, you could. If you could decide on one of these designs tonight, that would make things a whole lot simpler."

"I wasn't talking about the designs. I was talking about your dream. I have a lot of connections in high places and I can open some pretty big doors with my name." He put his hands on her shoulders, turning her to face him. "And I'd be glad to help out financially to get the ball rolling."

She stiffened beneath his grasp. Her eyes turned cold. "You know, until you showed up at my shop tonight, I wasn't even sure I still had you for a client. I worried that my harsh words would have you asking for your money back."

"I wouldn't do that," he said, drawing her closer. "I commissioned you to design a scope and that's what I want."

She pulled further away from him. "Good, because I intend to keep my end of the bargain. But I only get paid for what I produce. Nothing more, nothing less."

"I can live with that. But why can't I finance a small venture, sort of an investment?" His hands slipped from her shoulders as she completely turned to her sketches.

"No, thank you. I can make it on my own." She

quickly picked up her suede pouch and inserted the sketches one by one. "Everything I have, I've worked hard for, and I'm not about to compromise my convictions. Maybe you can just give up your dream without batting an eye, but I can't. I've set a course for myself and I plan to stick to it, however long it takes."

He felt the sting of her insult—he was a spoiled, pampered celebrity, unhappy with his life. She thought that fame and fortune should automatically bring serene happiness. It didn't work that way. He was proof.

"Sometimes we get blown off course and our dreams change." Slipping his hands into his pockets to keep them from reaching for her again, he watched her secure the pouch. "Maybe I just want something a little different than when I started out."

She turned and stared at him, long and hard, as though trying to read his meaning. He thought she was about to ask, but instead she tucked her bag under her arm protectively.

"Could we go now? I've had a very long day."

Janeen sat quietly in the back of the limo staring out at the chilly Boston night. Or was it just the chill of Georgios offering to use his money and influence to advance her career? In the five days they'd known each other, he'd managed to throw his money in her face every time they met.

As for his contacts, why shouldn't she accept that help? Did it really matter how she became successful? Yes, it did. She'd promised to return the money she borrowed from her father when she opened Chatter Box. He said there were no strings attached, but she'd insisted on paying it back, unlike her two spineless brothers who mooched off their father all these years:

lazy Tim who worked for Dad but did little; Robbie who spent every penny he earned and lost every job he had.

Janeen was determined to break out of the mold, to make her father proud. She wanted to prove that his only daughter was not a disappointment. His approval was a major factor in her struggle for success.

Georgios had fallen silent after he'd asked for her address to give his driver. As they cruised through Harvard Square, she noticed him staring at her out of the corner of her eye.

"Forgive my insensitivity back there," he finally said. "I have no doubt that you can make it on your own. You're a very resourceful woman. I just wanted to help any way I could."

Aware that she'd bruised his ego, she was sorry she couldn't bring herself to accept his offer. But how could she explain wanting something so badly to someone who'd never "wanted" in his life? To succeed, it had to be on her own terms, in her own way. Part of the victory was in doing it with no help, and she would allow nothing to stand in her way.

"I appreciate your offer, but this is my ball and I have to carry it all the way."

Through the darkened glass of the limousine, she watched the bright inner-city lights give way to the more subdued residential street lamps. Was Georgios's bright light about to diminish as well? She still couldn't imagine anyone giving up a successful career on a whim.

"So what will you do now?" she asked. "Do you really plan to give it up forever?"

The dim interior lights outlined his strong profile as he shrugged. "Forever is a long time. In some ways

I'll always have my music. But as it stands now, there's nothing to go back to. I'd prefer to go forward, start a new chapter." In a quietly suggestive tone he said, "I'm open to suggestions."

As the car turned up her street, she bit her lip apprehensively. Though relatively safe and quiet, her neighborhood was less than desirable, far from Georgios's status. The houses were old and in need of repair. Her apartment was the best she could afford while still feeling secure.

The car came to a halt in front of her building, double-parking the length of two cars. Once again, Tony opened the door on Georgios's side and Janeen moved forward to get up.

"Well, thank you for a lovely dinner."

Georgios held her arm. "May I come in?"

She sighed. "It's been a long day. I'm really tired."

"I never chose a design," he said, tapping her large leather bag. "Give me another chance."

Did he mean the sketches or something else? Either way, she really was tired. And she had to get up early tomorrow. But a part of her didn't want the night to end, didn't want him to go. She'd enjoyed his company and loved his deep voice. She wanted to hear more of it. She wanted more of his tender caresses and soft kisses.

Searching his eyes in the dim glow of the dome light, she detected honesty and sincerity. The chill in the air warmed as the corners of her mouth turned up in assent and he responded with a wide, flashing smile. Janeen tugged at her cumbersome leather bag, but Georgios reached over for it.

"Allow me," he said.

They both climbed out of the car and she briskly

led the way up the walk to the front stairs, then into a hallway she unlocked with two keys. Two sets of footsteps followed her. As she turned at the door to allow Georgios to enter, Tony's hulking figure reached the entrance.

"I can just imagine my neighbors seeing me come home late in a limousine, escorted by two tall, dark strangers."

"This is not normal for you?" Georgios teased.

"Not lately, anyway." She closed the door behind Tony and led the pair up the stairs. From the apartment on the right, the sound of Mr. Calzone's television suddenly went quiet. A finger to her lips, she nodded toward the door. "Shhh." She turned to the left and opened two locks on her door.

Janeen walked in, turned on the kitchen light, and waited for the men to follow. Georgios came in, but Tony took a position outside the door. "Is he going to stay out there?" she asked.

"Yes," he answered, closing the door without a second thought. "He'll be fine." Georgios set the leather bag down, but it fell over. He righted it, but it slid down. Finally, he picked it up and held it awkwardly, looking around for a suitable place to prop it.

"Don't worry," she laughed. "It never stays put. Stick it behind that chair near the counter. I'll be right back."

Quickly, she went to her bedroom to kick her heels off before her feet became permanently swollen inside her shoes. Slipping into her blue scuffed slippers, she returned to the kitchen where Georgios had seated himself at her little counter. Her feet were now comfortable but the rest of her was a bundle of nerves. How many months had it been since she'd invited a man into her apartment? Correction. She hadn't exactly invited him, nor had she turned him out. Regardless of how his need to always solve her problems with money continued to disquiet her, there was a powerful chemistry at work when they were together.

She went to a cabinet. "Would you like some coffee?"

"No, thank you. If you'll get the sketches out, I'll try to decide and then get out of your hair."

She closed the cabinet, disappointed that he truly wanted to leave. But his charming smile told her otherwise when she turned to face him. He was only playing along, trying to stick with the business at hand, just as she said she wanted.

A little more at ease, she pulled the suede pouch from her leather bag and spread the drawings on the counter. She brushed his shoulder several times as she ventured too close to where he sat. A tingle ran from the base of her spine to the back of her neck. *I have to be more careful not to touch him.*

Janeen stepped to the left and waited. Georgios rose from his seat and nudged back the stool. Starting from the right, he studied each sketch carefully until he reached the last one and bumped up against Janeen. She started to move over, but he extended his very long arm across her shoulders and drew her in.

"Why don't you help me out, give me a feel for your preference?"

She felt a sweat work its way up from her palms to her forehead. Her preference? She would prefer that he wasn't rich and famous. She would prefer that his eyes were less riveting, that just the scent of him next to her didn't shift her senses into overdrive, and that he didn't hold her so solidly.

Instead, amidst her confused reactions, she heard herself explaining reflections on stained-glass wheels, oil chambers, and mirrored images. The makings of a kaleidoscope were second nature to her. She didn't have to think about what she said.

"Musical notes?" he questioned, leaning his weight forward as he pointed to some writing on one of the sketches.

"Oh, yes, notes. I told you I was listening to your music while doing this. I thought some tiny musical notes floating in a colorful oil chamber would be nice. It was just a whim."

"I like it. Even before I saw that notation, I was leaning toward the oil chamber one. Yes, that's the one." He slipped behind her and placed reassuring hands on her shoulders.

"Good," she said. "And the wood cylinder?" His hands gently squeezed and released her shoulders. Her eyes closed.

"Perfect. I like wood. In fact, I might have liked to be a carpenter or something had I never become a musician."

His massaging hands worked their way down her arms, gliding smoothly on her cotton blouse. "Oh, really? You'll have to visit my father's wood shop some day. He's quite a craftsman."

Georgios lifted her hair away from her ear and kissed the awaiting strip of flesh exposed on her neck. "I'd like that," he whispered. "I'd love to meet all of your family."

Like a satisfied cat, she arched her back. Georgios wrapped both arms around her and placed gentle kisses all along her neck. She turned to meet his lips with hers.

Somewhere in the distance, through the haze of passion, muffled voices exchanged words. In her distracted state, Janeen caught only a word here and there: no . . . who? . . . police. Instinctively, she knew one of the voices to be her neighbor's.

Georgios raised his head. "It sounds like there's a problem in the hallway."

"It's probably Mr. Calzone giving Tony the third degree." A door slammed and she grimaced. "Maybe we should let Tony in," she murmured. "We don't want Mr. Calzone calling the police."

"Don't you think it would be a little crowded in here with the three of us?" he teased.

"Mmm. Right." She kissed the tip of his nose. "Then I guess you'll just have to leave."

He pouted like a child who'd just had a toy taken from him, but then he winked mischievously. "Then how about one for the road?" He bent her to the side and attempted a deep dip with his mouth following, but her fluffy slippers came right out from under her. Afraid she'd get hurt, afraid to let go, he clung to her until they both toppled over. His foot caught on her leather bag sticking out from behind the chair, which sent the chair flying across the room, landing with a thud against the door.

Instantly, the door crashed open. Tony stood there, legs spread, arms ready for battle. His eyes darted around the room, searching out the enemy. He finally spotted the couple on the floor, struggling to muffle their laughter.

"Are you okay, sir?"

"Fine, Tony. A little bruised, but fine." Georgios nudged Janeen. "How about you?"

"I'm okay. I landed on my padding."

"Very nice padding, I might add." He nuzzled closer for a kiss, then turned to Tony. "Thank you, Tony. I'll let you know if she gets too rough."

Georgios pulled her closer, but aware Tony hadn't left, he turned to him again. "Thank you, Tony," he stated firmly.

"Sir, a neighbor is about to call the police. He doesn't believe why I'm here and doesn't like me in his hallway."

Janeen sighed at Georgios's questioning look. "That doesn't surprise me. He's probably called the police already."

Georgios grunted and lifted himself off the hard floor, then offered a hand to Janeen. Once she was on her feet, he tugged her close and lovingly held her face in his hands.

"We don't want to upset the neighbors, do we?" He kissed her gently on the lips. "Besides, I promised to get out of your hair once I picked the design."

"I'm sure you'll love it."

He lifted her chin with a long finger. "I know I will."

Morning came slowly, as did Georgios's realization he'd never expected to be interested in Janeen Warner so completely. All too well he remembered the softness of her skin, her gentle curves, the smell of apple blossoms in her thick hair. He was drained.

Taking longer than usual with his morning routine, Georgios finally made his way down to breakfast. Tony sat at the round glass table in the kitchen, a black ceramic mug of steaming coffee in front of him, his face buried in the morning paper.

"Is my name in the obituaries?" Georgios asked.

"I avoid that page, sir."

"You'd better start looking. Between the way I feel this morning, and the fact that Michael Conway wants my head on a platter, it won't be long before my name is in there."

"Rough night, sir?" A slightly sarcastic tone seeped in to the usually emotionless sound of Tony's words.

Rubbing his spine where he had landed in his fall, Georgios answered, "In more ways than one." He shuffled over to the coffeepot and poured himself a cup. "Hand me the entertainment section," he said as he took a seat opposite Tony. "Let's see if the vultures have gotten wind of the decaying meat yet."

The two men read quietly, making no sounds except the occasional rustle of the newsprint as they turned the pages. Satisfied that the media hadn't caught up with his walkout yet, Georgios tossed the paper onto the table.

"Tony, you've been with me almost five years now, right?"

"It'll be five years in June."

"Do you think I'm crazy for what I've done?"

With his nose still in the folds of the paper, he replied, "It's not my job to second-guess you."

"No matter how many times I tell myself I shouldn't have done it, I can only remember how easy it was to walk away and how good it felt to know I was controlling my own life."

Tony continued to read. He made no comment, but then, he never did. He only answered when asked a direct question.

Georgios leaned into the table, thoughtfully cradling his mug in both hands. "What do you think of her?" he asked.

The newspaper went down. "Sir?"

"Janeen Warner. What do you think of her?"

Tony hesitated a moment. His eyebrows moved inward slightly. "I can't really say. She seems like a nice woman."

"She's a *wonderful* woman!" Georgios leaned back again. "She's beautiful, talented, intelligent. I feel I've known her all my life; I'd like to know her for the rest of my life."

Tony folded up the paper and placed it neatly on the table before taking a sip of his coffee. He lifted his narrow brown eyes to stare at his boss.

"I'm certainly not one to give advice about women, but you should give yourself a little more time to get to know her."

Georgios took a long gulp of coffee while staring at Tony. Getting to know Janeen Warner wouldn't change the intense feelings he'd already developed for her, but the process could be an enjoyable one. Yes. He'd show her he was as regular as the next guy, not just a flash in the pan.

He thumped the table with the palm of his hand. "You're absolutely right. Excellent advice, my friend!" He rose from his seat. "Go tell Gerald I want to leave in ten minutes."

It looks like a tornado hit this place! Janeen gasped at the shop's disorganized displays, the merchandise scattered about, and the scraps of wrapping paper left on the counter.

Was this Chris's way of getting even for leaving her alone in the store last night? Vindictiveness wasn't like her. On the other hand . . . Janeen looked down at the dark spot on the rug where her sandwich had landed. She was unpredictable.

Quickly dispensing of her coat and bag, she opened the safe and checked yesterday's sales. Not bad. As she slipped the drawer into the register, she saw the scribbled note.

Sorry about the mess. We were busy right up until closing. Holiday shoppers make me crazy! Luv, Chris.

That girl. Janeen laughed to herself. She gathered up the leftover wrappings and stooped to stuff them into the overflowing wastebasket. Raising her foot to squash the refuse down farther, she heard the door buzz and looked up to see Georgios enter. A smile as wide as the doorway lit up his clean-shaven face and shone bright against his dark complexion.

The shock of seeing him combined with her awkward stance threw her off balance as she pulled her foot out of the basket. Her arms went out to steady herself, one hand grasping for the counter, the other for a shelf behind her.

"I see we're continuing where we left off last night." Georgios smiled cautiously. "Do you need some help?"

"No. I just lost my balance for a minute." She kicked the basket back under the counter. Slowly, she dropped her gaze, hardly believing his casual black polo shirt and jeans. He looked so inviting. Her arms ached to hold him as she had last night—even more, she wanted him to hold her.

Embarrassed that the flush she felt would be noticed, she forced herself to change her train of thought. She peeked out the door and confirmed that Tony stood by as usual.

"What brings you here so early in the morning?"

"Bagels," Georgios said, holding up a bag from which oozed a moist, delicious scent of fresh-baked dough. "They're soft and warm." He placed the bag on the counter, quickly walked around it, and pulled her into his arms. "Like you." He kissed her slowly, tenderly. She remembered the passion of the night before, the tenderness of his words. She'd gone to bed intoxicated with excitement.

But this morning she'd sobered to the fact that she was playing a dangerous game. She had no time for a personal relationship right now. Her priorities were clear: keep the business above water, and get her kaleidoscopes marketed. A simple plan, but she was well aware of how many details were beyond her control.

Like my feelings for this man, she thought as he kissed her into blissfulness. Regretfully, she pulled away.

"Thank you for the bagels, and thank you for the compliment." She brushed her hands down her skirt and nervously straightened her blouse. "You'll have to excuse me. I have a lot of work to do. As you can see, leaving Chris alone last night wasn't such a good idea." She moved to the scarves and started folding and arranging them.

"I'll give you a hand."

"No!" Janeen surprised herself with her sharp answer. In a softer tone, she continued, "I mean, we shouldn't tempt fate. It seems that every time we're together something gets dropped or banged or broken. I can't afford any more of that."

She feared more for her own fragility than that of any merchandise, but she couldn't tell Georgios that. She needed to remind herself to treat him as a client, nothing more.

He murmured near her ear, "I promise to keep my hands to myself."

His hot breath sent a shudder through her. She couldn't think straight, she couldn't breathe. He was too close.

She turned away. "You must have better things to do than hang around here."

Chapter Seven

She could have kicked herself. Her nervous remark sounded more like a taunt. Of course he had nothing to do, he'd just given up his career.

Georgios casually opened the bag and took out a bagel. "Actually, I don't have a single thing I have to do."

He peeled back the wax tissue wrapping and studied the bagel a moment before taking a bite. His actions were so deliberate, so calculated. He really did have all the time in the world. "I'm sorry, that was insensitive of me."

Georgios smiled. "Hey, don't worry about it. I chose to leave. No one forced me."

He put down the bagel and carefully wiped his hands on a napkin while she distractedly draped a red and gold scarf on the metal rack. Before she knew it, his hand covered hers.

"Now I have time to do what *I* want to do."

Again, Janeen pulled away. "Georgios, please don't misunderstand me. I enjoy your company and wish we could spend more time together. But I just don't have the time to spare. Right now my whole life is this shop. On top of the long hours, I have to put together a presentation for Neiman Marcus next week, and I only have four weeks to complete your kaleidoscope."

"Why can't I help?"

"You're paying *me* to do the work, remember? And by the way, we haven't settled on a price yet."

He waved his hand. "Price doesn't matter. I just want the best kaleidoscope you can create."

She sighed. "And you'll get it, as long as I can devote the time needed to the project."

His eyes narrowed as though considering his options. "I can't change Mother's Day, but surely there must be something I can do to help take the pressure off."

She shook her head. The disappointment on his face squeezed her heart. She saw that he sincerely wanted to help, but there was nothing he could do. The designs were done. Now it was just a matter of the inner workings and her father's wood casing. Of course, she still had to get the sketch to him. . . .

"Okay. You really want to help?" she asked.

His face brightened again. "Absolutely."

"How about if you take the sketch over to my father so he can get started on the wood?"

"Great! Anything else?"

"No. That'll be enough to get production going and save me travel time." She went to her leather bag and took out the design Georgios had selected. She held it up before putting it in a manila envelope. "Are you sure?"

"Positive."

"Okay." She scratched some instructions on a note for her father and inserted it with the sketch. Then she began another note with directions to her father's shop. "This is where he is. It takes about twenty-five minutes unless you hit traffic. Tell him this is the job I spoke to him about on Sunday."

"You told him about me?" His tone was suggestively hopeful.

"No," she reprimanded him. "I told him about a custom kaleidoscope. Now get going so I can get some work done."

He took the envelope and directions from her, slid his hand to the back of her neck, and pulled her close for a kiss. "We'll make a great team."

"Mr. Warner, please." Georgios couldn't ever remember being so nervous about meeting someone.

"Which one?" The pleasant-looking, middle-aged receptionist peered suspiciously over Georgios's shoulder to where Tony lurked in the background.

"I beg your pardon?"

"Which Mr. Warner?" the secretary clarified.

He was stumped. He had no idea. "There's two?"

"Three. Howard, Tim, and Robbie."

The envelope had no name. Flustered, he explained, "I'm supposed to deliver this to Janeen Warner's father."

"One moment, I'll page him." She picked up the phone and pressed the intercom. "Mr. Warner, please come to the office." Smiling briefly, she turned back to her computer.

The paneled walls, large oak desk, and three dark gray metal filing cabinets implied a simple, long-established business without a lot of frills. Yet modern touches such as the phone system and electronic office equipment all appeared up-to-date.

Off to the left was a window to the woodworking shop. Beyond that were rows of machinery, piles of sawdust and wood chips, stacks of wood panels, pallets of work in process, and jigs and forms for shaping or cutting every conceivable product.

A man in his fifties with salt-and-pepper hair walked over to an air hose. He quickly blew the dust off his tan work pants and blue plaid shirt. Casting a glance through the window, he proceeded to the door that connected the office to the plant.

The secretary nodded her head toward Georgios. "Howard, this gentleman is here to see you."

"Mr. Warner, your daughter asked me to deliver this." Georgios handed over the manila envelope.

Howard Warner glanced out the front window while opening the packet. He squinted his eyes slightly, as though not quite believing what he saw, then shifted them to the corner of the room where Tony waited. "Things must be pretty good at the Chatter Box for Janeen to send a limo and . . ." He hesitated, then nodded toward Tony, "security?"

Georgios smiled. "No. I'm just doing her a favor."

Janeen's father turned his attention back to the contents of the envelope and read the note. "Oh, yes. The kaleidoscope." He stuffed the papers back into the envelope, then stuck out his hand. "Thanks for bringing this. Tell Janeen I'll get right on it." He turned to the door.

"Uh, excuse me, Mr. Warner?" Georgios fought an oppressive feeling of being a schoolboy asking a father permission to take his daughter out.

Howard Warner faced Georgios. "Yes?" He waited patiently while tongue-tied Georgios struggled to find words. "Oh. Sorry." Reaching into his pocket, Mr. Warner pulled out some bills, offering them to Georgios. "Here. Thanks again."

"No! I wasn't waiting for a tip." Georgios wanted to crawl out of his skin he felt so foolish. He'd embarrassed the man while making himself look like an opportunist.

Well, maybe he was, but for a different reason than Mr. Warner would have guessed. "I'm sorry to trouble you like this, but I've always been interested in woodworking." *What I'm really interested in is your daughter.* "I was wondering, would it be possible to get a tour of your plant?"

Later that day, Janeen's father called her. "I really had to search to find a good piece of birdseye maple."

"Great, I was afraid you'd be out of it." Janeen knew that asking for specialty woods was pushing it, but her father usually came through. "What about the quartersawn oak?"

"No problem. I had a few planks left over from a job a few months ago. The walnut, I always have."

"Wonderful."

"Why do you need so many samples of the same barrel?"

"Because I want to be sure to get the right look, but I won't know which one is best until I finish the stained glass."

After a slight pause, her father asked, "I liked your friend. Have you known him long?"

"He's the client, Dad. I sent him over only because he's in such a hurry for the scope and he offered to help."

"It's the first time I ever had a limo parked in my lot. I had to chase everyone away from the windows to get back to work when he left. What does he do?"

"He's a musician." She avoided an explanation of his fame. With little interest in music, her father would have no idea who Georgios Andros was.

"Why don't you invite him over for dinner Sunday?"

"Dad, this is a business relationship. I'm designing a scope for him and I need you to rush it along. With the tight deadline I don't even know if *I'll* be there for dinner."

"Yeah, he told me."

"He told you? Why would he mention the deadline?"

"Oh, it just happened to come up in the conversation."

"What conversation? He was there to drop off a sketch." Janeen didn't like the sound of her father's lighthearted tone.

"We chatted a bit while I gave him a tour," he explained.

Oh, God! She shouldn't have trusted them together, no telling what else was said. After all, her father would like nothing better than to see her safely married to a handsome, rich man who could take good care of her.

On the other hand, she couldn't tell her father why she was bending over backwards to get this scope finished. She'd never let on how bad business had been or how close she was to closing the shop. All she'd ever wanted was to prove that at least one of his children could succeed on her own. Unafraid of hard work, she'd do whatever was necessary to meet that goal.

Janeen sighed, regretting that she'd sent Georgios on the errand. She wouldn't let it happen again. "Dad, I've got customers coming in. Call me when you have something ready."

She hung up the phone and looked around the empty store. The customers would be coming in any time now.

Two days later, Georgios slipped into the gift shop while Janeen waited on a middle-aged couple. She caught the flash of his smile as he casually approached the chessboard display.

While she demonstrated a music box to the couple, she noticed Georgios pick up a porcelain chess piece. Remembering their last costly encounter with the chess pieces, she sent him a hard glare to serve as a warning. He gently set it back down with a shrug of his shoulders and a shy smile. It was then that she noticed the brown carton he awkwardly carried in his left arm. He probably wasn't used to carrying his own things, she mused, glancing out the door at Tony.

The couple finally made their decision and left with their gift-wrapped purchase. As Janeen put away the paper, Georgios approached and placed his box on the counter in front of her.

"Special delivery," he announced.

He was too close, too close to refrain from touching, too close for her to miss his scent of mint. To ignore the desire for his kiss and the warmth of his embrace would be to deny every ounce of her womanhood. Something about his presence never ceased to excite her. Her only hope was to do her best to control it.

She opened the carton and saw three wooden cylinders for the scope project. "Where did you get these?"

"From your father," he explained. "He says to take a look at them. He can still make some modifications if needed."

Speechless, Janeen just stared at Georgios, trying to make sense of what he said. "What are *you* doing with them?"

"He called me to say they were ready."

"You? Why? How did he get your number?" Janeen had a strange feeling of helplessness, as though she'd been flying a kite and the string had just slipped from her grasp.

"We had a long talk the day I delivered the sketch and I gave him my card. I offered to shuttle the samples back and forth. He does nice work, and what a great shop."

The kite was far from view now. When had she lost control?

"So, how do they look?" Georgios asked impatiently.

"I won't know until I get them home. I've been working on the stained glass for the last two nights."

"How is it going?"

"Slow. It's tedious work. I have to pick up more lead on the way home."

"Let me get it for you," he offered.

"No, it's right on my way."

"I don't mind, really. It'll save you a step. Remember, you promised to let me help. This will give you more time for the creative part."

Janeen's helplessness now weighed heavily. She'd forced herself to stay up late the last two nights working on the glass wheels. When she had finally fallen into bed, she couldn't sleep, thinking of warm kisses and strong arms.

"What time are you leaving?" He interrupted her thoughts.

"As soon as Chris gets here. In about an hour and a half."

"Look. I have to stop at my mother's restaurant. I'll do your errand, take you home, then grab some take-out food from her and come back to your apartment. I'd like to see what you've done so far."

That would mean having him in her apartment again, a very reckless move. On the upside, it meant a comfortable ride home in a limo instead of a crowded train. Her tired feet wouldn't have to walk those extra two blocks to get the lead. She wouldn't have to cook and she'd get his feedback on the scope.

It all sounded so appealing and she was too tired to argue. Sighing, she said, "Okay. I'll write down what I need."

Janeen buzzed the downstairs door open after Georgios called on the intercom. She heard the multiple footsteps on the stairs and pictured Tony shadowing Georgios. But to her surprise, she opened the door to find Georgios standing with a tall handsome woman, her dark hair in a neat bun with a large white streak running from front to back. She had Georgios's dark eyes, olive complexion, and undeniable presence.

"Janeen, this is my mother, Odessa Andros. She insisted she had to deliver her food herself."

Janeen realized her mouth was open and only closed it when the smiling woman stepped forward after possessively taking the bags from Tony's hands.

"That's right. I had to see the woman who has so captivated my son that he broke a dinner date with his mother."

Janeen sent a stricken look to Georgios, pleading to help her out of this. "Oh, Mrs. Andros, I'm so sorry, but this dinner really wasn't necessary. Georgios didn't tell me—"

Mrs. Andros held up her hand and smiled mischievously. "Not to worry. A mother is only too happy to know her son has found someone more important than a graying woman." She handily unpacked the containers of food and placed them in the center of Janeen's tiny table. At the same time her eyes roamed the small apartment, as though appraising Janeen by her decorating. "You have a delightful little place here."

"Thank you. Please sit down and join us."

Again, the hand came up and her face lifted in an aristocratic manner. "No, I can't stay. I must get back to the restaurant." She sighed heavily. "Sometimes it consumes me, but it's all I have since my Theo left this world ten years ago." She slipped past Georgios and turned to pat his cheek. "That and my little Geo."

He kissed his mother's cheek. "Thank you for the food, Mother. I promise to stop by in a few days."

Mrs. Andros rolled her eyes. "He says that all the time. It's all a mother can hope for." And then she was gone.

Georgios closed the door, shrugged at Janeen, and they both burst out laughing. Without fanfare, they started digging in to the cartons of the exotic cuisine feast disguised as take-out.

After light conversation and many mouthfuls of wondrous food, Janeen sat back from her little kitchen table that overflowed with containers of Greek food. Everything had been delicious—the moussaka, the souvlaki, and especially the baklava. She couldn't remember the last time she'd eaten so much food at one sitting.

"Your mother is a wonderful cook." She wiped the buttery remains of baklava from her fingers.

"She doesn't do as much of the cooking as she did when my father was alive. Running the restaurant takes up most of her time, but she oversees every detail, especially the cooking."

Janeen peeked in several of the open containers. "There's so much left over. Why don't you ask Tony if he'd like some? After all, he helped carry it up."

"I sent Tony and Gerald off for a few hours. They'll get themselves something to eat."

"You mean you're here alone, without a bodyguard?" she asked sarcastically.

He leaned forward. "I have you to protect me."

"And suppose I'm the one who is the danger?" The relaxed atmosphere and good food had put her in a playful mood.

Georgios ran a long slender finger down her nose, stopping at her lips. "I'll take my chances."

Slowly, he moved in for a kiss. His lips felt warm and tasted of the sweetness of baklava. She smiled as a picture of their last time in her kitchen flashed through her mind. "Okay, but I'm warning you. I have a chair that can be deadly."

They both laughed heartily. When she rose to start

clearing the table, he stopped her with a hand over hers. "Why don't you get started on your work. I'll take care of this."

With a grateful smile, Janeen collected her supplies from the other room and returned to see him packing the refrigerator.

"Your fridge is as bare as mine," he commented.

Janeen set her supplies down on the breakfast counter. "I would've thought yours would be packed with food all the time. Don't you have servants?"

He retrieved more containers from the table. "Just a housekeeper who does everything from laundry to cleaning. No cook. I usually eat at my mother's restaurant or carry in something when I'm not on the road."

"And Gerald and Tony," she reminded him.

"They're more like business expenses than servants."

Janeen stopped. "A business you're not in anymore."

Georgios closed the fridge door. "Right."

Yes, he was definitely out of the business, as definite as his attraction to this lovely woman with the lustrous brown hair that swirled around her shoulders whenever she moved.

Janeen had resumed her set-up work. Her fingers nimbly sorted small pieces of glass, the lead Georgios had brought, and the soldering iron with its own special hot pad.

"So will you be discharging them?" she asked absently.

"Tony and Gerald? Not yet. I'll see what happens when things quiet down." He took a seat on the stool next to Janeen.

"You mean, you'll wait to see if you get back into music." An emphatic statement, but he heard the question behind it.

"No. There's no more music left. It's all been played out." The only music he heard now was Janeen. Being around her was like being at a concert. A symphony of sound reverberated in his head whenever he kissed her. The sounds brought him to life and he liked the new feeling.

Now, as she precisely put her soldering iron to the glass and lead, he wanted to take her in his arms and cover her tempting, smooth neck with love bites. He wanted to make beautiful music, with her.

As though hearing his thoughts, she lifted the iron from her work. "This requires a lot of concentration. If you can give me about ten minutes, I'll show you how it all goes together. Then we'll see how the barrels look with the glass."

He conceded to a short intermission in the concert.

"They're too long." Janeen groaned. She wanted to show Georgios how the kaleidoscope went together, to impress him with her artistry. But the cylinders were too long. When she slid the mirrors inside there was too much space at one end, which showed up as a black splotch through the viewing hole.

"Does that mean your father has to make new ones?"

"No." She pulled the viewing end apart and removed the mirrors. "He can sand them down and rebevel the opening. It just means we're at a standstill for a few days."

"Why? It can't take long to sand and bevel three barrels."

"No. But I'm working right up to closing both tomorrow and Saturday. The soonest I'll get these to him will be Sunday." As soon as she'd said it, she knew what was coming next.

"I'll take them over tomorrow," Georgios offered. "I can wait until he's done and get them right back to you."

No. She couldn't take the chance of letting her father loose on Georgios again. Or was it the other way around? Either way, the thought of them together without her supervision was too frightening. No telling what they'd cook up.

"No. It'll have to wait until Sunday. Even if I got them back tomorrow, I wouldn't be able to work on them."

"Why not?"

"I just told you. Chris is off; I'm working all day and night for the next two days."

"Oh, right." Georgios looked thoughtful for a moment. He picked up the little stained-glass wheel she'd made, turning it slowly while studying it. "I still don't see how three of these wheels will turn independently once they're mounted."

Janeen took the wheel from his grasp and set it down gently. "That's why I'm making the scope and you're not." She jumped down from her stool, ready to gather up the parts.

Georgios grabbed her arm and pulled her toward him. He stared into her eyes. If she'd wanted to pull away, she couldn't. He'd locked his fingers behind her and his dark eyes never left hers. The reflection of the wall lamp sparkled like a star in his pupils. Looking deeper, she saw a hungry want.

"I'm not questioning your talent," he whispered. "I know you can do it." He moved one hand to stroke the hair at her temples. "And I admire your artistry. You show so much determination." He kissed her lips gently while settling his fingertips along the side of her throat.

She allowed her own hands to come up to his shoulders. Her fingers sought the back of his neck and she ran them through his thick hair, enjoying the feel of the silky waves. His kiss deepened. Their mouths danced in a harmonious waltz.

As he lifted his mouth from hers, he brought his other hand around to tenderly touch her face. He stroked her jaw. His hypnotizing eyes captivated hers while he spoke close to her mouth in a husky voice.

"Let me bring them to your father." He kissed her again when she started to protest. "Let me be a part of the project."

Once more she tried to speak, but another kiss stopped her. "Let me be a part of your life." He kissed her hard, as if to emphasize his meaning.

She heard footsteps in the hall and then a light rap on the door. "Tony must be back," she murmured against his lips.

"He can wait." Georgios hugged her close, rubbing her back with one hand and resting his cheek on top of her head. "I don't know how much longer I can, though."

She'd never felt so wanted. His sincerity moved her, and his gentlemanly manner touched her. She sensed a wall falling down somewhere inside her. His offer made sense. If he brought the cylinders to her father the adjustments could be made quickly without wasted time. Instead of worrying about insecurities, she needed to concentrate on important matters. He was the client. Give the client what he wants.

"If I let you bring them to my father, do you promise not to listen to anything he says about me?"

Georgios lifted his head and flashed her a sly smile. He raised his right hand. "Promise."

She studied his innocently masked face for a moment, then broke free from his embrace. Picking up the wood parts, she placed them in the carton, then quickly snatched open the door. Tony nearly tumbled into the room.

"Tony, would you personally deliver this to my father tomorrow and see that Mr. Andros says nothing more than hello and good-bye?"

Tony looked to his boss for help, but before Georgios could respond Mr. Calzone opened his apartment door across the hall. "What's all the noise out here? Oh, it's you again!"

Janeen smiled reassuringly. "It's okay, Mr. Calzone. They're just leaving. Sorry to have bothered you."

In the limo, Georgios opened the glass panel. "Gerald, Quincy Market, fast!" *Before Chatter Box closes,* he thought.

Georgios fell back heavily against the seat, drained by the gamut of emotions he'd experienced over the last few hours with Janeen. She made his heart pound, his knees weak. She also made him take a hard look at himself. He knew he'd done the right thing walking out of the recording studio, even though it had been spontaneous. He'd lost the passion for his work.

But he saw that passion in Janeen. She took hold of her talent and played it out loud, full volume. He smiled to himself. If nothing else, he'd see that her direction remained steady.

It seemed as though only minutes had passed when the car came to a halt on a side street. Georgios walked swiftly through Quincy Market with Tony close behind. In seconds, the men descended the stairs to the sub-level gift shop.

Chris looked both surprised and confused when Georgios hurried in. "I thought you were with Janeen."

"I was." He scrutinized the display of scopes just as he had done the first day he'd come into the shop, only this time he knew what he wanted. "I want to buy some kaleidoscopes."

"I was just about to close up."

"Well, you have one more sale to make. Would you open the case?" He heard the terse tone of his voice and instantly tried to cover it. "Please."

Chris picked up the keys, seemingly unaffected by his momentary sharpness. She opened the case and, pushing the curls back from her face, asked sweetly, "What would you like?"

His finger extended, he pointed through the glass. "That one, that one, and . . ." He brought his finger to his lips. He couldn't remember the third one Janeen had said was a best seller. *Seascape.* "That one."

Chris's mouth opened wider with each choice. "You want all three?"

"Yes." He smiled to himself. He would've bought all twelve if he didn't think Janeen would get suspicious. But with her tied up in the store the next two days, he'd make some connections, even a quick trip to New York.

Chris began wrapping the scopes carefully. "Isn't Janeen designing a special scope for you?"

"Yes, she is."

"So, why are you getting three more?"

Georgios looked down at the tiny girl with the enormous head of hair. He smiled, reached for her chin, and tipped it up so he could look into her eyes. "I would like this to be a secret between you and me." He lowered his voice to a conspiratorial level. "Can you do that for me?"

She stopped wrapping and stared at him, unblinking. "Uh, I guess so." She swallowed hard.

"Good." He released her chin and thought he heard her sigh. "Now, what's the total?"

Chris finished her wrapping and added up the purchases while Georgios counted his money. "Hmm. I don't have enough cash and I can't write a check because Janeen will see it." He pulled out his charge card. "Here, put it on this."

Shaking her head, Chris protested, "No, she'll see that, too. She checks everything in the deposit envelope. An amount that large, she'll look at the name on the slip for sure."

Georgios thought hard. If Chris would keep the store open, he could get to an ATM. But he'd feel guilty asking her to wait when she was ready to go home. Yet he didn't want to wait until Janeen wasn't working again. Suddenly a thought hit him.

He turned. "Tony! Do you have a charge card?"

"Yes, sir." Tony seemed ruffled by the personal question.

"Bring it here." Janeen would never recognize Tony's name.

The transaction completed, Georgios thanked Chris for her help and pressed a hundred-dollar bill into her palm.

"Remember, this is our secret."

With a gasp, Chris stared at the bill in her hand. "I can't take this!" she whispered.

"Of course you can. You are a superb salesperson and that is your tip."

"Thanks," she murmured.

"Now how about a ride home in a limo?"

Chapter Eight

J aneen reluctantly looked at the clock. She had fifteen minutes to catch the train to her parents' house for Sunday dinner. Given a choice, she'd rather stay home and lounge in a sweat suit, sketching, listening to some music. Like the night she'd sketched the scopes to Georgios's music. It had been the first time in a long time she'd felt so connected to her art.

Speaking of Georgios, she hadn't seen him since he left Thursday night. She'd come home Friday night to find the familiar carton from her father sitting in front of her door with a note. She knew the handwriting from the check Georgios had written the day he'd walked into her shop and her life.

Didn't have time to leave this at the store, had some business to take care of. Hope the modifications work. It was signed, *G.* followed by *P.S. Mr. Calzone's really a nice guy.*

Janeen had laughed to herself, picturing Mr. Calzone in his slippers and T-shirt answering the door to the sophisticated Georgios Andros. He'd obviously charmed Mr. Calzone enough to leave the package, which was a major feat in itself.

The timer went off, startling Janeen from her thoughts. She went to the oven to remove her famous chocolate-chip nut bread. Its sweet aroma filled the small apartment with a warmth it'd been missing for many busy months. Her father loved this bread, so she had decided to surprise him with it for being so patient with her scope demands.

Trying not to think about what had transpired between Georgios and her father, Janeen set the bread on the cooling rack. She then inspected the scope cylinders one more time, carefully testing the mirrors for fit. Each one slipped in perfectly, but the end caps didn't quite sit tightly. Her father must have used a different bit to bevel them. She knew it'd be no problem for him to redo them if she brought them along. After dinner they could take a quick ride to his shop and make the adjustments.

She gathered up all the components, wrapping the glass and mirrors carefully, and packed everything neatly in the box. As she wrapped up the bread, her door buzzer rang.

"Yes?" She spoke into the intercom.

"Hi. May I come up?"

Georgios. What was he doing here? "Hold on."

Stealing a quick look in the mirror near the wall lamp, she pinched her cheeks and smacked her lips together for some quick color. With both hands, she fluffed up her hair at the temples, and then made a mocking face at her reflection.

"It'll have to do." Janeen slung her purse over her shoulder, picked up the box and nut bread, and carefully made her way down the stairs to open the entry door.

Leaning against the doorjamb, Georgios leveled his smiling eyes at her. "When I woke up this morning, I thought, 'What would be the best way to spend this beautiful spring day?' " He reached out and ran the back of his finger along her jaw. "The answer was obvious. I should spend it with you."

Her face tingled where he'd touched it and her pulse raced inside her veins.

Even though his romantic charm had an undeniable effect on her, she reminded herself to stay focused on her work. She needed to keep her emotions in check.

"Perhaps you should have consulted me first," she reprimanded him. Brushing past his tall frame, she stepped out onto the porch. "Could you hold this?" After handing him the warm nut bread, she locked the door behind her. "I'm on my way to my parents' house."

"Okay." He didn't appear too disappointed. "This sure smells good." He began to lift the plastic wrap off the bread, but Janeen quickly rescued the dish from his grip.

"This is going with me."

She started down the steps and he followed closely. She turned right at the sidewalk and saw his sleek black limo waiting. He motioned a hand toward the car.

"I told you, I'm going to my parents' house," she said firmly.

"I know. I'll take you."

Janeen hesitated. A tempting offer. Without a car of

her own, she'd gotten used to the train and walking. When she took the train to her parents' house, the closest stop was six blocks away and she usually didn't mind the walk. But today, with the extra burden of the box as well as the bread, a free ride sounded wonderful.

Or would that be flaunting her arrival in a limo for all the old neighborhood to see? No, she assured herself. She was merely accepting an offer.

They climbed into the limo and it pulled away from the curb immediately. "If you'll open the glass I'll tell Gerald where to go," Janeen said, frowning at the control panel of buttons.

With a secretive smile, Georgios said, "He knows where he's going."

That strange feeling of helplessness came over her again and she didn't like it one bit. She was about to ask his meaning, but suddenly a more important question came to mind when she realized Gerald was alone in the front seat.

"Where's Tony?"

"I gave him the day off."

"What?" she asked in astonishment.

"He's been working very hard. A day off will do him good." He tapped the box in her lap. "So, how did the modifications work out?"

"Good. They just need a few quick adjustments, nothing drastic."

"Uh oh."

"Uh oh, what?"

"I . . . hope it wasn't something I did." The sheepish look on his face said he'd been caught with his hand in the cookie jar.

"Why would it have anything to do with you?" She sensed that she really didn't want to hear the answer.

"Your father let me run the bevels on them. What a great feeling, working with wood."

Janeen sent him a cautious look, unsure if he was pulling her leg. "He let you run a machine?"

Georgios nodded. "He's a wonderful teacher. He explains everything so well. I felt like I knew what I was doing before I even did it."

This couldn't be. Her father never let anyone other than trained employees use the equipment. First of all, the liability of anyone running the machines, or even being in the shop, was prohibitive. Second, he never let anyone work on his special projects.

Something didn't sound right. There had to be more to the story. She would get to the bottom of it later. For the time being, she sat back and watched the familiar scenery, which somehow looked different through the tinted glass of the limo.

At the Warners' home, Gerald pulled the limo into the long, narrow driveway. Janeen's father pushed open the squeaky screen door of the back porch just as Georgios got out of the car.

"Glad you could make it!" He clapped Georgios on the back as they shook hands heartily. "If we waited for Miss Independent here to invite you, I might be in a wheelchair."

Janeen stopped dead in her tracks behind the men, who were already walking into the house. "You invited him?" she shot back.

"Sure. He's become such a regular at the shop, feels like he's family." He held the door open for the young couple to enter. "Come on, your mother is dying to meet him."

The next hour passed with Janeen only half-hearing the spirited conversation. What she did hear was her parents gushing about her superior attributes to a prospective husband for their unattached daughter. She heard her brothers ask questions about music and celebrity with open admiration. And she heard an inner voice scold her for allowing him to come. Her attraction to Georgios was hard enough to fight by herself. But with the whole family on his side, she feared it would be a losing battle.

As the women cleared the table and the men left the room, Janeen's mother spoke softly. "I wouldn't mind having *that* man at my table every week. He's so polite and sophisticated."

Janeen continued stacking and rinsing dishes in silence. She'd made her non-relationship with Georgios perfectly clear, and if she planned to keep up the facade, she'd better hold her tongue. Her feelings for Georgios were hard enough to hide from herself. The last thing she wanted was to acknowledge her confusion in front of the family.

She listened as her mother rambled on about how nice it would be to have a famous son-in-law and how Janeen could live in the lap of luxury.

No. She wouldn't give in. Let them think what they wanted.

Her sister-in-law added, "He's so handsome. Janeen, however did you catch him?"

With a clatter of dishes on the countertop, Janeen looked straight at her brother's wife. "First of all, I didn't catch him. He's a client, that's all." She lowered her voice and struggled to speak calmly without clenching her teeth. "I'm making a kaleidoscope for him. When it's done, he'll go back to being his normal, rich, famous self. I'll go back to being a shopkeeper." Janeen paused to take a deep breath. She could feel the veins pushing against her temples as her blood raced to keep up with her runaway anger.

"Oh." The wimpy woman grunted. "I just thought dinner with the family meant more than a business meeting."

"Well, it doesn't, especially when *I* didn't invite him." In an attempt to calm down, Janeen busied herself by rinsing a sponge in the soapy dishwater and mechanically wiping the splatter marks off the stove. It struck her that what bothered her most was everyone's concern over her love life, or lack of one. Like the sponge, the real Janeen had numerous nooks and crannies, hidden niches that no one saw or knew about. She liked her privacy and wanted to keep it that way.

Turning quickly, she pointed the wet sponge at her sister-in-law. "And furthermore, who says I couldn't catch someone like that if I wanted to?"

"I didn't mean it that way, Janeen. I just meant—"

"Never mind. It doesn't matter. Dad's the one who invited him here, not me. Like I said, he's just a client."

At the sound of approaching steps Janeen turned back to her cleaning task. She'd said more than she'd intended. It wasn't like her to react so harshly to silly remarks. A lot of what she did lately wasn't like her. Was this what Georgios did to her? Had her firm grip on her tightly reined life slipped because of one charismatic man who kissed like he'd invented it?

"Anything I can do to help?" Georgios's deep voice made her hand tremble as she wiped at a stubborn gravy spill.

Oh, goodness! Even the sound of his voice affects me.

Janeen's mother answered him. "No! You just go in there and watch the sports channel with the men. We're almost done here."

"I'm afraid if I sit any more, you'll have to pry me up with a crowbar." He groaned. "I ate far too much and the good cooking is to blame."

Janeen raised her eyebrows as she heard her mother giggle with delight. Did he have to charm everyone?

He continued in a lower voice. "Actually, I was hoping Janeen would help me walk off a few calories."

Her mother snatched the sponge out of her hand. "Go on," she said in a hushed tone. "We'll finish up."

Janeen thought about refusing, but fresh air and a change of scenery held much more appeal than the stale kitchen conversation. She reached for a towel to wipe her hands, then briskly turned, heading for the back door without a word.

Georgios caught up with her on the back porch and reached for her hand. "What's your hurry?"

She withdrew her hand and defensively crossed her arms. She wondered why she had to continually fight herself, why she was always on the defense. Why couldn't she relax and let herself fall in love? Other women had jobs and careers and managed to find love. They married, had kids, and achieved success. Why couldn't she?

Because I don't know any other way. After her brothers' failures, she'd programmed herself for achievement. The cost was a lonely life.

They walked silently to the back of the yard where her mother had an assortment of potted spring plants lined up in the sun. She found them reassuring. Knowing those beautiful flowers would bloom again, as they always did, gave Janeen a sense of security, something sorely lacking in her life lately.

"I like your family," Georgios said softly.

She wondered about his meaning. Had he expected not to like them? "They're okay in small doses."

"Ah, but you'd miss them if they weren't around."

"I suppose. But I also know I can love them from a distance too."

"You'd only be cheating yourself."

They walked to the edge of the yard and stood at the chain-link fence that separated them from the field where the power lines ran. With her arms against the sharp metal fence, Janeen turned to Georgios suddenly. "Why are you doing this?"

"What?" he asked, puzzled.

"Coming into my family, acting like we're an item."

"I didn't realize I needed your permission to accept an invitation from a friend," he explained softly, his dark eyes squinting slightly. Was it from hurt or the glaring sun?

"My father invited you because he thinks throwing us together at a family gathering will set the wheels in motion." Janeen turned her gaze back to the field. How odd it looked with its overgrown shrubs popping up everywhere—not at all like the wide open field of grass where she and her brothers had played many years ago.

"What wheels?"

Janeen sighed. "The wheels that make a woman want to settle down, raise a family, bake bread."

"And you don't?" he asked.

Did she detect a hint of disappointment? "Not right now. I told you, my dream is to have my own line of scopes, to sell them in prestigious places, to be known for my art. Until then, marriage is not even on the dream list."

He'd settled on the fence too, right next to her, leaning his arm against hers. "So you've sworn off men." It was as much a question as a statement.

"No. I just need all my time to concentrate on my work."

Georgios reached for her hand. He looked at it as though making an examination. "And having a man in your life would distract you, right?"

"Yes." His gentle touch against the backs of her fingers sent a wake-up call throughout her body. She yearned to bring his hand to her face, to feel his strong male skin against her soft, receptive cheek. But she had to resist her desires and instead pulled her hand away.

He put his other hand on her shoulder, turning her toward him. "Sometimes, if you focus on something else in your life, you free the creative juices from their restraints. You can be a successful artist and still enjoy yourself, you know."

Afraid her resolve would not hold up, she dropped her eyes from his entrancing stare. "It doesn't work that way with me."

He lifted her chin with a gentle finger. "I think it could if you gave it a chance."

He lowered his mouth to touch her lips. She closed her eyes and accepted the moist warmth that would surely leave her wanting more. She found it so easy to move into his arms and embrace the tall strong fig-

ure. Her hands stroked his back, feeling the smooth-
ness of his white polo shirt. Beneath the soft material
was a hard muscular body that seemed to promise
everything she could ever want in a man.

He raised his face away from hers and looked longingly into her eyes. "I'd like you to give me that
chance, Janeen. I don't think you realize how much
of an effect you've had on me this past week and a
half. I feel like I've known you all my life instead of
a mere eleven days." He framed her face with his
hands. "Not one of those days has gone by when I
don't think about you. You've caused me many restless nights trying to figure out how to have you all to
myself."

He planted another searing kiss on her waiting lips.
His enticing words were as smooth as his lips. She
wanted to go limp in his arms and beg him to take
her away to a land of enchantment. She found herself
drifting dangerously close to the edge of commitment
and, strangely, it didn't seem to matter whether she
fell off the ledge or not.

A crisp spring breeze kicked up and her hair flew
in her face. Georgios worked his fingers through the
strands to set them back in place.

"If you would let me, I could make things easier
for you, give you more free time to spend on your
kaleidoscopes."

Janeen jerked her head back as though she'd been
slapped in the face. *He's talking about paying me off
again!* She glared at him, unable to formulate words
that weren't venomous. She wriggled herself free from
his grasp and paced to the edge of her mother's garden. She kicked at the mint plants that bordered the
mulched soil. The fresh scent wafted up, reminding

her how much she loved the smell of Georgios's cologne. It was a scent she would always remember. A scent she had to forget.

With a deep intake of breath, she turned to face him as he approached her. Struggling to remain calm, she began, "Up till now, I have done very well juggling my free time and my work. I'm sure with a little self-restraint and discipline, I can continue with my plans for success. By myself."

She took a step back to make it clear she didn't want him to touch her again. She couldn't chance having his kisses sway her from her sound decision.

"If you are so determined to spend your money, I'm sure there are any number of charities that would gladly accept. But Janeen Warner is not a charity case."

Georgios watched her turn and walk back toward the house—away from him. What had he done? The woman who had come to mean everything to him, whose mere presence started his blood flowing more rapidly, was walking away from what he had hoped would be the beginning of his new life.

It was becoming painfully clear to him that money was not the means to all ends. Too often he'd used money to solve problems or get what he wanted, but it would not work with Janeen. He realized money was not the way to get her, in fact it seemed to be the one thing that turned her away. Even though his intent had been to help her, to make things easier, he hadn't taken into account the strong will and determined pride of this stubbornly independent woman.

Obviously no explanation would make any difference now. He'd lost all points he'd gained and he was afraid she might not let him back in the game. He needed a new strategy.

"Janeen!" Mrs. Warner called from the porch door as they approached the house, Georgios following slowly behind. "Janeen, Chris is on the phone. She has a question about a stock item."

As Janeen got to the phone and instructed Chris where to find what she was looking for, Georgios shuffled into the living room to join the men in front of the TV.

"Well-ll, back already?" Howard Warner seemed pleased that Georgios had joined them. "Where's Janeen?"

"She's on the phone talking to Chris at the store." He hoped he'd disguised his bruised feelings. He didn't want his mood to affect Howard Warner—he genuinely liked the man.

"That girl. She lives and breathes that store. It's a wonder she takes time out on Sunday to have dinner with her family." Mr. Warner got up and went to the box of scope parts Janeen had brought. "I want to talk to her about the changes we made. Were they all right?"

"I think so. We really didn't discuss them much. I've been tending to some business the last few days."

His private time at the piano really wasn't business. For the first time in a long time it had become pleasure. After purchasing the three kaleidoscopes from Chris Thursday night, he'd sent Tony to New York with two of them. The third he showed to his contact at Neiman Marcus. After delivering the box to Howard, he'd spent almost every waking hour tinkering with new scores at the keyboard and looking into the scope.

He felt so close to Janeen when he viewed the miniature fantasies she'd created, the same magical feeling he got whenever they were together. She tried to deny it, but he knew she felt it too. To her this was business; to him it was living.

And even though she wasn't with him in his music room, there was a oneness between the beauty he saw in her scope and the music that played in his head. It became louder as the colorful geometric shapes cascaded nonstop before his eyes. He was driven to play the notes, to write what he felt.

What he felt was freedom—freedom to love, freedom to live. The keyboard didn't scare him anymore. Though he once found it threatening, he now approached it willingly, already anticipating the music that had begun in his head. And it was all about Janeen, for Janeen. His music had never been so focused. Rediscovering the joy of composing was exhilarating.

He had hoped to share this feeling with Janeen when he went to her house that morning. But from the moment she'd opened the door, things hadn't gone as he'd expected. Instead of connecting on a creative level, he was standing here listening to her father's laundry list of solutions for minor technical problems.

"The caps don't quite fit right. I think the bevels need to be run again. That bit we used must've been off a hair." Mr. Warner moved some things around inside the box and said, "Why don't we take a ride to the shop and try it out now?"

"Try what out?" Janeen asked, entering the room.

Her voice was stern, her gaze steady on the box. Her brothers, Tim and Robbie, momentarily lifted their eyes from the baseball game to see what the commotion was. They probably guessed that their sister was not in the best of moods and quickly returned their attention to the TV.

"The changes that need to be made on the scope barrels. I suggested we run over to the shop and try them out." Howard Warner didn't seem to catch the meaning behind his daughter's icy stare. Georgios was all too aware of what it meant.

"We? Who is we?" she asked, her arms folded tightly.

"Me and George. It'll only take a few minutes."

Georgios took a deep breath. He feared the storm that had been brewing was about to break over his head.

"Your father says the bevels need to be run again."

"Oh, he does? And I suppose you agree? Nice of the two of you to consult me. After all, I'm only the designer." Janeen went over to her father and retrieved the box from his grip. "If you want to go make the adjustments, fine. But I'm going too."

Chapter Nine

"This is the first time I've ever been in a limousine," Janeen's father proclaimed in awe. "I always figured I'd ride in one at my daughter's wedding. But, marriage seems to be the farthest thing from her mind." He looked out the window, escaping the harsh glare Janeen directed his way.

For Georgios's benefit, who was seated across from them, Janeen replied, "You'd think he'd be satisfied having his two sons married, even though Robbie's didn't last."

"That's not the same," her father interjected. "A father wants to see his daughter taken care of, safely married to a good man. Don't you agree?" He sought out Georgios's approval.

Georgios cleared his throat. "I've never really given it much thought. As an only child, my experience with fathers and daughters is limited." He was clearly uncomfortable.

"Why can't a woman provide for herself?" Janeen shot back at her father, as though Georgios hadn't even spoken. "You struggled and made it, don't you think I might want to do the same?"

"I know it's not hip to think like this, but I see nothing wrong with a father wanting his daughter in the safe care of a good man." Mr. Warner let out a little huff as though he'd said his last word on the subject.

But Janeen hadn't. "Regardless, I won't get married till I'm good and ready, and certainly not to be taken care of."

Out of the corner of her eye, she saw her father study Georgios for a moment before he turned back to the window again. Minutes later they arrived at the plant and talk of marriage was replaced by the loud hum of the blower system being turned on.

"Janeen, turn on the compressor while I set up the router."

Years of helping her father in the plant had given her plenty of experience with the equipment. After turning on the compressor, she deposited her box on a nearby workbench and removed the wooden cylinders to be modified. Georgios had been watching her father, but now he came to join her.

"I'm sorry for upsetting you earlier. My only intention was to help if I could. Please understand my sincerity."

"I know your offer was sincere. I'm just a little funny when it comes to having things given to me. I need to succeed on my own. There's nothing you can do to change that, any more than I can help you with your music. We each create in our own way. I assume you also need your space and solitude."

He reached for her shoulders, turning her to face him. "With one major difference. I have room for other interests."

She stared into his dark eyes. "That's because you quit the one thing that drove you all these years. You were good, you succeeded, then you just dropped it like a dirty sock."

Her sharp tone made him tighten his grip on her shoulders, but she refused to acknowledge their closeness. She wouldn't give him that advantage. She needed to keep up a strong front.

"I didn't drop it." He clenched a fist over his heart. "It's still here, deep inside. It has always been a part of me and it will never leave. But I realize I've reached a point in my life when other things should take priority."

"Like what?" Her question was a challenge. To her, nothing could be more important than success.

Georgios didn't answer. Instead he raised his hand to her face and warmed her cheek with his palm. The fire in his eyes burned into her soul. More than anything, she wanted to look away so as not to admit her own needs, her own desires. How could she not want him? How could she not let him into her life? She was losing her perspective.

"Okay, you guys. I'm all set."

Her father's voice intruded on their silent, intimate exchange, but Georgios kept his hand against her cheek and his eyes steady. Janeen moved first, tearing herself away from his riveting gaze. Inwardly, she knew she was doing the right thing, though a part of her ached to forsake everything and accept the love he offered. *But not now,* she told herself. *I have work to do.*

She brought the cylinders to the router her father had set up. Georgios followed, slowly. They watched her father test the movement of the pieces behind the cutter.

"Hmm. I probably should change this fence. It's all chewed up." He pointed to the nicks and gouges in the hard maple piece. "Otherwise we'll get bumps in the bevels." He unclamped the board from the work-table. "George, go grab a piece of maple out of that scrap pile. I need a piece about the same size as this. You can cut it on the table saw over there."

Georgios left without a word. "Dad, his name is Georgios," Janeen whispered.

"Same thing."

"And why are you letting him run machines?"

"Don't worry. He's fine."

Janeen sighed. No matter what she said, her father had it set in his mind that Georgios was going to help. She went back to the workbench for the box of parts. Behind her, the table saw whined as Georgios cut the board her father needed.

A moment later, the unmistakable grinding sound of wood binding in the blade stopped her. Then, the high-pitched zing from wood being kicked back made her whirl around. She heard the block smack the floor and saw Georgios holding his hand.

Both she and her father raced to the table saw. Georgios's hand was already covered in blood. He stepped back from the machine, his stance a little shaky, his face white.

"I think you'd better get me to a hospital," he said, gasping.

* * *

As she applied gauze to the huge gash in the web between his thumb and forefinger, Janeen tried not to think about the possibilities, even while Gerald raced them to the hospital.

As soon as they wheeled Georgios into the emergency room, Gerald called Tony, then left to pick him up. The hospital staff was sensitive to Georgios's celebrity status and whisked the Warners to a private waiting room. Janeen did her best to answer the questions, but she had to wait for Tony to fill out forms with any accuracy.

Guilt began to eat away at her composure. She should've trusted her instincts and not let Georgios accompany her to her parents'—even worse, she should've insisted he not run a machine. On the other hand, if she hadn't been so heartless when he bared his soul, he might not have been distracted at the saw.

There were too many ifs and not enough answers.

Now, as she sat helpless, waiting for the doctors to work their miracles, the thought of what had happened sickened her.

"Miss Warner?" She felt the presence of a hulking figure beside her before she actually heard the question.

"Tony!" She jumped up, throwing her arms around the large man. When he stiffened at the unexpected greeting, she quickly released her hold and sat down. Tony took a seat opposite. "Someone in admissions needs to speak with you about forms and his medical history."

"I know, I took care of it already. They discreetly took me aside to avoid any commotion and have agreed not to issue any public statement."

Janeen smiled through tear-filled eyes. "I'm so glad you're here."

"I shouldn't have left him today," Tony murmured.

"Don't blame yourself. You had a well-deserved day off. If it's anyone's fault, it's mine."

"No. I'm supposed to make sure he's safe, from himself as well as outside danger."

"Look, it happened. All we can do is hope for the best."

Janeen's father stood by the window, staring. She went to his side. "Dad, why don't you go home. There's no sense in all of us sitting here waiting. Gerald can drive you."

Her father's forlorn face tugged at her heart. She knew he too was blaming himself. "Are you sure?" he asked.

"Yes, Tony is here now. Gerald will drive us home later."

The next two hours seemed like days. Tony read magazine after magazine. Janeen alternately paced and sat down until she finally had to say something. "I suppose it's a good thing he quit the music business. An injury like this could've been a terrible setback."

Tony squinted his eyes. "Is that what he told you?"

Fear shook Janeen from head to foot. Had Georgios lied to her? Had he in fact ruined his career with this injury that resulted from her thoughtlessness? She tried to remove the sweat on her palms by rubbing them together. "Are you saying he didn't?"

Tony put down his magazine. "No. He did walk out of his recording session and he told his manager he was through."

"Then, what? What are you saying?" Her voice rose with the panic.

"I'm saying I don't completely believe him. I think I know Georgios Andros better than anyone, even himself. Music means too much to him to just drop it for good."

"So, you think he'll go back to it?"

He nodded. "I heard him tinkering with the keys last night. It's just a matter of time. He has some things to work through but he'll be back. One thing I'm good at is judging people."

A doctor exited from the double doors with the red NO ADMITTANCE sign. "Are you Mrs. Andros?"

Flustered, Janeen replied hastily, "No! We're just . . . friends." Feeling a blush creep up her neck, she quickly turned to Tony. "This is Tony, his body-guard."

The doctor looked back and forth between the two as though deciding who should receive the diagnosis. "We've closed the wound and did our best to repair some tendon damage. Mr. Andros can go home, but he needs to see a specialist in a few days, after the swelling goes down."

"How serious is the damage?" Janeen asked.

"I'm afraid I can't answer that. He'll have to see the specialist. Whatever the outcome, he has an extensive recovery period ahead of him."

Janeen accompanied Georgios home to reassure herself as much as to be there for him. Exhausted from the ordeal, he dozed for most of the ride to Wellesley, which seemed to take forever. The light outside faded as had the color in his face.

The limo finally turned uphill into a long, winding driveway. When a door opened to an underground garage bigger than her entire apartment, she felt as though she'd slipped into a dreamworld. Janeen stared at her surroundings.

As Tony helped her, then Georgios out of the car she noted a red foreign sports car, a white convertible Mercedes, and a waiting room sealed off by a wall of glass. It housed plush furniture, a TV, and a built-in stereo system.

Tony led the way to an elevator and pushed a sequence of numbers on the digital pad. They rode in silence but Georgios seemed to perk up when they reached the foyer of his home.

Janeen had prepared herself for the shock of luxury, but she was more shocked to discover the opposite. Big bucks had obviously been spent on decorating the bachelor pad with its thick carpeting and flowing draperies, yet it was far from overdone. Only a few pictures adorned the walls and the furniture was tasteful, yet comfortable.

"I'll order some food," Tony said before he left the room, disappearing down a long hall.

"I'm sorry that it took a stupid accident to get you to my home," Georgios said. "May I show you around?"

"No. You should get some rest. You've had a traumatic experience." She felt uncomfortable in his house, like an intruder in his private world.

"I'm fine, really. They shot me with enough anesthetic, I won't feel a thing for hours." He reached around her shoulders with his good hand. "Come on. Come see my room."

Janeen stiffened. The last thing she wanted to deal with right now was being alone in a bedroom with this man who shook her to her very core every time they were together. So much had changed. She'd had lots of time to think and realized his need to control her was in complete opposition to her own needs. Even without the complication of his injury and her guilt over it, she knew she couldn't put herself in this predicament.

"No." She stopped mid-stride as he ushered her along a short hallway. "I can't."

"Can't what?" Georgios asked, puzzled.

She inhaled deeply. "I just wanted to be sure you were okay and to see you settled in. I really should be going."

"Please. Just take a look at my room." He stretched his arm toward the doorway where they'd stopped.

She peeked in, embarrassed as she saw a huge room that would be the envy of any musician. Filled with an assortment of speakers, keyboards, and other electronic equipment completely foreign to Janeen, the room was unlike anything she'd ever seen.

She stepped in. The ceiling and walls were covered with a blue padding like that in sound rooms at radio and TV stations. In the far corner, two steps led up to an alcove where a magnificent black piano stood surrounded by windows screened with sheer white curtains. It looked like a shrine to a genius.

Of course. This was his room—his music room.

"This is where I create. What do you think?" Pride laced his words. Everything he needed was in this room.

"It's fabulous. Do you really use all this equipment?"

"At one time or another, yes. I can virtually call up an entire symphony and transfer it onto one master tape while I'm composing. Modern technology is a wonderful thing."

She walked to the center of the room and scanned

the shelves that held hundreds of tapes and sheet music. The wall leading to the alcove displayed photographs of Georgios shaking hands with celebrities and politicians. One picture caught her eye. Georgios at a much younger age sitting at a huge piano, flanked by his mother and most likely his father.

"Is this your father?" she asked, pointing to the dark frame, but it was hardly a question she needed to ask. He was the spitting image of his father, but with his mother's smile.

"Yes." He quickly closed a drawer and joined her in front of the photo. "That was my first public concert. Can you see my knees shaking?" he laughed.

"How old were you?"

"Fourteen, and proud as a peacock. I'd lived a somewhat sheltered life—private schools, music lessons. I thought I was ready to take on the world after that concert. The applause resounded in my ears for days." His voice dropped to a more somber tone. "I guess that's what all performers live for—applause."

"You don't sound very enthusiastic about it in retrospect."

"As thrilling as center stage is at the beginning, it eventually wears on you. You begin to wonder how long it will last and if the applause is genuine. I think artists have a crazy kind of self-destructive gene."

Janeen understood that. All during her college days, she was never quite sure if her work was good enough. She'd always felt the only recognition that counted was from her peers.

She stepped up to the beautiful piano. It shone as black as Georgios's hair, the ivories as white as his smile. She let her fingers trail along the smooth surface as she edged herself between the keyboard and the bench and sat on the hard seat.

"Do you play?" Georgios asked.

"No. I couldn't even manage a scale if I tried."

He scooted next to her, gently placing his bandaged hand on her far shoulder. "Sure you could. Here." With his good hand, he took her fingers and touched them to the keys one at a time, playing the seven notes of the scale. "Now you try it."

She tried, but began on the wrong key. He took her hand again and started the scale. She felt his breath against her ear as he mouthed the notes in a whisper.

This was what she'd been afraid of. This was the contact she wanted to avoid, though her body craved it. Something in the electricity of his fingers warmed her cold resolve. Her rigid posture relaxed and she leaned against his strong chest.

"Not everyone was meant to be a musician," he assured her. "But with a little practice, anyone can learn the basics."

When she lifted her gaze from the keys, she noticed a musical score resting on top of the piano. It had pencil marks in the margins, notes crossed off here and there, and strange symbols everywhere that meant nothing to her. What caught her attention was a printed "J" at the top.

"A new composition?" she asked, fingering the crisp sheet.

He hesitated. "Something I've been tinkering with."

Tinkering. That's what Tony had said. "What does the 'J' mean?" She felt his breath close to her neck, as though he were trying to inhale a scent.

"It's just a letter." His husky voice ended at her lips. He took her mouth hungrily, unexpectedly.

She felt a searing energy course through her veins. The fire on his lips burned deeply. They kissed long and hard and time skipped by.

Janeen almost forgot her flimsy reasons for keeping their relationship on a business level as she wove her fingers into his dark wavy hair. She thought about his injury and how he still managed to kiss her so thoroughly. But the thought quickly vanished. He didn't need two hands to kiss her.

Suddenly, his head became still in her hands. His kisses had stopped. She looked up at his face now white and covered with perspiration. His expression seemed stricken with distress. This was not the look of passion, she thought, as she felt his body go limp.

Georgios's ears buzzed as though tightly stuffed with cotton. His vision was spotted with black, gray, and white splotches. With a weakness he'd never experienced, he staggered to the bathroom which, luckily, was just off the music room.

Once inside, he clung to the vanity to steady himself. Struggling with one hand to dampen a cloth under running water, he brought the cool wetness up to soothe his hot cheeks. Though his face was warm, he felt chilled all over. He had no idea what had come over him, but he knew where it was leading.

He lunged for the commode and let the unnatural reverse process run its course. With each heave, his head pounded more and more until the throb became almost deafening.

When the nausea subsided, relief washed over him in a cold wave. He slumped to the floor, hugging his knees to retain his body heat and control the shivers. The doctor had warned him about nausea, but why did it have to happen in the middle of the most wonderful kiss he'd ever experienced?

A light rap on the door. "Georgios? Are you all right?"

Janeen. How could he face her? What kind of man leaves a woman in the middle of a kiss to throw up? He raised his hands to his head to smooth his disheveled hair. The unfamiliar feeling of the bandaged hand jarred him for a moment.

"Yes," he answered, his voice betraying his weakened condition. "I'll be out in a minute." Maybe. He knew it would take him a full minute just to pick himself up off the floor.

Mustering all his remaining strength, he raised himself up and leaned on the vanity, waiting for his head to stop spinning. With his good hand, he splashed cold water on his face, then rinsed out his mouth. He studied his wan reflection in the mirror. *Is this the face a woman could love?*

He loved Janeen more than anyone he'd ever known. She triggered excitement in his secluded life, bringing out feelings that filtered up to his brain and down to his nimble fingers. Her kaleidoscope, which he'd barely had time to hide while she'd looked at his photographs, had awakened his sleepy creativity. "J" was the first composition with any merit he'd written in months. He longed to finish it and play it for her. But. . . .

He looked down at his injured hand. Strange how you don't appreciate something until you've lost it.

Georgios wiped his face with a towel and went to the door, turning the knob slowly. He expected to see Janeen standing there, but she'd vanished. Taking in the entire music room, he saw she was nowhere to be found. He tried to hurry toward the kitchen, but his wobbly legs hampered his progress.

He heard voices coming down the long hall from the elevator and looked up to see Janeen and Tony walking briskly toward him.

"Sir, are you all right?"

"Yes, Tony. I'm just a little weak and tired. I guess all the excitement was too much for me." He exchanged a look with Janeen. She knew exactly what excitement he was talking about.

"We should get you to bed." Tony lent a supporting arm.

"Wait." Georgios stopped. "I need to talk to Janeen."

Tony nodded and obligingly left them alone in the kitchen.

"Why don't we sit down?" Georgios didn't trust his legs.

Positioning his chair at the table, Georgios faced Janeen, their knees almost touching. He reached for her hand. Its warmth felt good in his cold fingers. Her eyes were warm too.

He breathed slowly, deeply. "I want to apologize. . . ."

"Don't be silly," she interrupted him. "It's not your fault."

"I feel as though everything that happened today was my fault. I only wanted to be with you and have a good time."

"We did." Her low voice didn't sound very convincing.

"No. I made a mess of everything. You were right, I shouldn't have forced my way into your family." Her slender fingers felt so soft. He wanted to touch them to his lips, but restrained the urge. He needed to keep his thoughts clear. "My bumbling offer to help was done with the best of intentions."

She leaned in closer. "I shouldn't have been so harsh." Her voice sounded pained and her eyelids batted away tears.

"It's all right. I respect your independence. And this," he held up his injured hand, "this is what I get for thinking I'm some kind of woodworker."

"Don't be ridiculous." Janeen's voice suddenly had that fire in it again, the fire that burned from her soul. "Even professional woodworkers get hurt. It wasn't your fault that the wood bound up in the blade."

He chuckled softly. "Thank you, I think. Anyway, please tell your father not to worry. I have full medical insurance, and no one will know that the accident happened in his shop."

She smiled cautiously and rose from her seat. "I really should be going. You need to get some rest."

Willing strength into his legs, he stood and engulfed her in his embrace. "What about us, Janeen?"

"What do you mean?" she murmured.

"What happened tonight was more than a kiss and a spark. It's not something I can forget. And if you're honest, I don't think you will either." He held her tightly, looking down into her eyes that suddenly seemed clouded with fear. Georgios forgot about the pain in his head and the pain in his hand. What he felt now was a stabbing pain in his heart.

"I. . . ." Janeen averted her eyes. "I have to go. Could you call Gerald to take me home?"

Chapter Ten

Monday morning was anything but routine for Janeen. She tallied the weekend sales without seeing the numbers. She checked the inventory list but couldn't decipher what needed to be ordered. She waited on a few customers with a far-from-enthusiastic sales pitch. All she could think about was Georgios—his passionate eyes, his kisses, his caresses.

His injured hand.

What if Tony was right? What if he'd been destined to return to music? What if he was unable to play again? The burden of guilt was unbearable. She'd been around the shop long enough to know how easily accidents happen; she should've stopped him. It was one regret she'd have to live with forever.

The other regret was their relationship. She shouldn't have let it go so far; she shouldn't have misled him. Her first responsibility was to her career. She'd told him as much at her parents' house, as well as her need to succeed on her own.

Strength was the key. She had to stay strong in order to maintain her independence, but more important, she had to keep her distance from Georgios. For whatever reason, it seemed bad things happened to him because of her. His lost interest in his music, his fight with his manager, his accident. Maybe she needed to be strong for him, let him get his life in order without her distraction.

Certain that was the best for both of them, she decided against any visits or phone calls. The night before, she'd asked Tony to call her with an update in the morning. Dependable as ever, Tony called early to say Georgios had slept well, though he'd awakened a bit on the grouchy side. He had an appointment with the specialist the next day.

"Tony, I can't see him for awhile. He's already called the store, but I let the machine answer. I need some time to think and get things straight. I know it's unfair to ask, but can you tell him for me? Tell him I'll be thinking of him and working on his project, but I must be alone."

"I understand, Miss Warner."

"Thank you, Tony. Would you mind keeping me informed though, about his hand?"

"Of course, Miss Warner."

As the hours passed, she busied herself with simple tasks in the store. It was all her tattered nerves could handle. While dusting the displays, she looked into the kaleidoscope cabinet and noticed three were missing. She remembered the high sales total from Thursday that she had never asked Chris about. She did recall one large charge slip though. No doubt Chris would be bursting to tell her all about it when she got there.

Chris arrived, smiling as usual but cautious. "How was your day with the folks yesterday?"

Janeen considered spilling all the horrible details, but she couldn't burden the sweet girl with her grief. More important, everything would lead to the accident, and she at least owed Georgios his privacy. Who knew what the media would make of the story if it slipped out?

"Oh, the same. Arguments, tension, the men watching sports. Same old, same old," she answered reticently. Anxious to change the subject, Janeen asked, "Chris, I noticed there are three scopes gone. Did you have a big sale?"

Chris turned her back and fiddled with the display of scarves. "Uh, yeah. It was pretty busy Thursday night."

How odd that she didn't gush with all the information. "So one person bought all three?"

"Yeah, weird, huh?" She abruptly turned around. "Can I go grab a soda before you leave? I'm dying of thirst."

Yes, it was weird, and Chris obviously wanted to keep it a secret. Too tired to ask her for any more details, and certain that she'd eventually spill the beans, Janeen agreed. "Sure, go get your soda. I'll be leaving in a few minutes."

Like clockwork, Tony called Janeen every day to keep her abreast of Georgios's condition. He had day surgery on Wednesday and the specialist was hopeful for a speedy recovery. By Friday, he'd started therapy and everything was going well.

Relieved, Janeen sent flowers and a card, then focused her attention on her kaleidoscope presentation for Neiman Marcus. Though the ten-minute sales pitch went perfectly, she couldn't read anything on the buyer's face. He thanked her and said he'd be in touch.

With that out of the way, she then concentrated on Georgios's kaleidoscope and finished it by the following Thursday. Everything fit together perfectly. The three stained-glass wheels were the best pieces she'd ever done. Each wheel had variations of a primary color: one in reds, one in blues, the third in yellows. The wooden barrel shone with the luster of four coats of hard lacquer, giving depth to the distinct markings of the birdseye maple. The oil chamber had sealed up without a flaw and it brilliantly displayed the tiny crystals and miniature musical notes afloat in their sea of harmony.

Janeen stared at the scope on her kitchen counter, then at the phone. The professional thing would be to call her client to set up an appointment for delivery. She would have to be polite and ask how he was doing, even though Tony had told her that morning how daily therapy was having a remarkable effect on Georgios's recovery. The thumb had regained almost half of its full range of extension.

"And, I heard him on the piano last night," Tony had continued. "My rooms are just below the music room. Whatever he was playing, he was persistent about getting it right."

Janeen had been surprised to hear Tony share this information. She was beginning to understand just how important the two men were to each other.

She picked up the scope and looked through the lens. As she turned the glass wheels, she knew she'd captured the spirit of his music. Tiny notes floated in colorful backgrounds, surrounded by shimmering gems. The scope was perfect. It was Georgios. It was her best piece ever.

She hurriedly picked up the phone and dialed the number on the business card in front of her. On the sixth ring, his machine picked up. ". . . at the tone, please leave a message."

Janeen's hand shook as she waited for the beep. "Hello, this is Janeen Warner. I'd like to set up a time when I—"

"Hello!" His husky voice instantly stilled her heart.

"Oh, hello." She swallowed hard. The lump in her throat felt the size of an orange. "How are you doing?"

"Pretty good. I had some minor surgery last week and the doctor says I'm doing better than he'd expected."

"Great. I'm glad to hear that." She knew they were toying with each other. She knew that he knew that she knew. "I called to tell you I finished the scope."

"Wonderful. When can I see it?" His enthusiasm was not what she'd expected. Irritation at her avoidance of him would've been understandable. Anger that she refused to speak to him personally for a week and a half would have been explicable. But excited? Warning bells went off in her head.

While a little voice inside her said, *You know what will happen if you see him,* she heard herself saying aloud, "Tomorrow. Can you come by the store tomorrow?"

"Oh, no, I can't. I have several appointments tomorrow, plus therapy. What about tomorrow night?"

"I'm not working tomorrow night."

"Perfect. Then you can come to my place for dinner."

His mellow tone set her skin tingling. *Don't do it,* the inner voice said. Janeen closed her eyes. "I can't."

"Why not? You said you weren't working." His words demanded an explanation.

"I don't want to start something I can't finish."

"We've had dinner at your place, now it's my turn. You owe me." Was he talking about dinner, or her desertion that Sunday night? Even worse, was he playing on her guilt over his injury?

Whatever his meaning, something in her heart said, yes, he's right. You owe him.

Friday dawned with the promise of summer-like heat in the city's maze of gargantuan buildings. By noon, Janeen had unfastened the top button of her blue blouse and pulled her hair up to dry the dampened tendrils at her neck. The air outside was stifling as the strong May sun baked the cobblestones. At her stool behind the counter, she tried to think of cool foods and cool places but every thought evaporated as her real concern surfaced—how would she handle herself tonight with Georgios?

Absently, she wrung her hands. She could think of no way to back out. Not only did she owe him a kaleidoscope, but her moral support and compassion.

The sound of the phone ringing next to her made her jump. "Chatter Box. May I help you?"

"Janeen Warner, please."

"This is Janeen."

"This is Walter Allen with Neiman Marcus. I've gone over your proposal and I'm interested in purchasing some kaleidoscopes, particularly your 'Sea-scape.' I think it would do well with our seafaring clientele in the summer months."

Janeen could hardly believe her ears. She'd peddled her scopes to all the major stores in Boston and every shop on Newbury Street. Finally, a bite.

"I should have a few in stock which I could get over to you the first of the week."

"I'd appreciate that. I'd also like to discuss a custom kaleidoscope for a new Oriental theme we're developing in our gift line. Would you be interested?"

Interested? It's what I've dreamed about all these years. It's recognition, acceptance, validation! "Yes," she answered calmly. "Do you have a deadline?" Not that it mattered.

"No, I have some leeway on the project, but I'd like to sit down with you as soon as possible to get the ball rolling."

Before hanging up and nearly doing a back flip, Janeen scheduled a meeting early in the week. She caught herself smiling the rest of the afternoon. Riding home on the train, she was oblivious to the pressing, perspiring bodies around her. The unseasonable heat had long since stopped bothering her. She walked down her street with a spring in her step, her head held high. Confidence boosted her up the stairs to her apartment.

Now, if it can only get me through the night, she thought as she closed the door.

Gerald picked Janeen up promptly at seven-thirty. By the time the limo entered the underground garage, her earlier elation had solidified into a huge knot in her stomach.

Clutching the simple gift box containing the kaleidoscope, Janeen followed Gerald to the elevator. An apprehensive shiver ran through her when he waved her in and nodded good-bye as the door closed between them.

Upstairs, Georgios heard the elevator signal and took a deep breath. This was the moment he'd waited for all day. This past week and a half he'd ached for Janeen, wishing he'd told her how much he loved her instead of getting sick that night. He would make things right tonight. They belonged together.

As the elevator door slid open, he scooped up two glasses of champagne and went to the foyer to greet her. He stopped in his tracks at the vision of loveliness that stepped out.

She looked cool on this hot night in a peach silk top with a scoop neck and short sleeves. The loose material was cinched at her waist by a belted beige skirt. Her shapely legs winked at him from the tips of her low-heeled pumps to the tops of her knees.

"Welcome." With shaking hand, he offered Janeen a glass. "To the loveliest thing I have set my eyes on in over a week."

Janeen smiled cautiously, as though searching for words to return the compliment. Her wavy brown hair was pulled up off her face and neck with a ribbon that matched her blouse. She tucked a gift box under her arm and accepted the glass, taking a tiny sip in response to his toast.

Georgios went to her side and started to slip his left arm around her waist, but she somehow turned out of his reach and touched the hand that now sported only a simple gauze bandage.

"How is the hand doing?" she asked simply.

He tried not to show his disappointment at her rebuff. "Pretty well. As painful as the therapy was at first, its benefits are quite noticeable now. Look." He held up his hand and rotated the thumb.

"Does it hurt?" Deep concern marked her voice.

"Not really. Once in a while I get twinges of pins and needles, but the doctor says that's normal. The nerve endings are working to reattach themselves." He moved to her side again and put his hand at her back this time. "Let's go sit."

He led Janeen to the living room. His gray sofa, love seat, and chairs looked so mundane now as her breathless color splashed the simple room with life. While the black tables and lamps accented the plain white walls, she was a sprig of springtime amidst the stark masculine decor.

As he sat beside Janeen on the love seat, he lowered his gaze to the box in her lap. "May I see it?" he asked eagerly. They both put their glasses down on the table in front of them, knuckles brushing ever so briefly, awakening all his nerves.

She proudly handed him the box. "I hope you'll like it."

"I know I will," he murmured as he flipped the top off the box and pushed aside the tissue paper. Freeing the scope from its wrappings, he raised it to his eye and aimed it at the light. The colorful notes struck him at once. He gasped in awe as he turned the wheels, first all together, then separately, and viewed beauty and music brought together with love.

Janeen stirred in the seat next to him. "Well?"

Georgios continued to move the wheels slowly, taking in every triangular burst of color that came to life before his eyes. He couldn't help but see her heart and soul in the refractions. He knew she'd put this together with more love than she was willing to admit.

When he finally lowered the scope lens from his eye, he carefully placed it on the table with the drinks. He turned to Janeen, gazing into her striking blue eyes. He couldn't speak. He could only stare as her slowly blinking eyelids enticed him ever closer. He thought he felt a breeze from the soft brown lashes. Each blink drew him closer. Closer.

Janeen wished she could silence the pounding of her heart inside her chest. From the moment she'd stepped out of the elevator and the smell of fresh, warm bread had permeated her nostrils, she'd had a feeling of being under Georgios's spell. He'd dressed casually in dark blue pants and a baggy, light blue print shirt. The collar was open down to the third button, exposing his inviting chest. Now, sitting so close, it was all she could do to keep her fingers from touching it.

Georgios had been staring at her in a most unnerving way. She was afraid he might not like the scope, but with a flash of recognition, she knew he saw where the scope had come from. It came from a place in her heart few people saw, a place that was warm, safe, and loving. A place she'd been saving.

He moved closer, slipping his arm behind her back, pulling her to his broad chest. Her body went limp in his embrace as he lowered his mouth to singe her lips.

Georgios suddenly lifted his mouth but kept his lips against her cheek as he whispered, "Except for what I'm holding in my arms, I've never seen anything more beautiful."

Relief washed over her like a gentle wave. "I was so afraid you might not like it."

He tipped his head back. "By now you should know me better than that. I know beauty and talent when I see it. You've created the essence of music in a tiny cylindrical world."

"Well, it was your music that inspired me." She fought to stop her voice from shaking. "I merely captured what I heard."

"Seeing my music gives it a whole new meaning." He smiled in a most engaging way.

"I hope your mother likes it."

Georgios drew back, stood up, and pulled Janeen to her feet. "The heck with my mother. This is mine." Once more, he kissed her fully, generously, with a quiet sigh. After a gentle hug, he softly whispered in her ear, "Come on. Dinner is waiting."

Janeen started with surprise when Georgios plopped a bowl of spaghetti and meatballs on the table.

"Sorry. I'm not much of a cook, but at least I did it myself. Sort of. The meatballs and sauce came from my mother's restaurant. And the bread."

Janeen laughed. "It's the thought that counts."

"I made the salad on my own, though, which wasn't easy with this thing." He held up the bandaged thumb.

They ate, exchanged lighthearted small talk, and gazed longingly into each other's eyes. Now and then Janeen noticed a serene little smile. She wished she knew what he was thinking.

After a brief silence, Georgios commented, "Not that I'm complaining, but you look different tonight. Happier."

She lowered her gaze and smiled. "I didn't think I was that transparent." Lifting her eyes to meet his again, she inhaled with pride. "I have some good news."

He continued to smile, waiting patiently for her news. How could she put into words the jubilation she had felt since that afternoon? It was so personal. He might not even find it anywhere near as exciting as she did. "Well, what is it?"

Her smile spread with her growing excitement. "Neiman Marcus wants to put one of my scopes in their store, and they'd like me to design one for their new line of Oriental giftware."

"No wonder you look different. Success becomes you."

"I could hardly believe the call was real. I feel like it's all finally coming together."

Georgios rose from his chair and pulled her up for a giant hug. "I'm very happy for you." He planted a reassuring kiss on her forehead. "Your persistence has paid off."

Together they cleared the table and loaded the dishwasher.

"Let's take our coffee into the music room," Georgios said. "I have something to show you." He led them to the room and set his coffee on a counter that looked like it served as a desk area. He went to the wall that held numerous shelves of digital equipment and pushed buttons and levers until soft sounds filled the room from speakers that seemed to be everywhere.

Janeen listened to the beautiful notes of a piano searching out her heartstrings. A strange feeling of familiarity came over her, but she didn't understand why.

He suddenly hit a button that turned off the music. "What do you think?"

Stunned that he should ask her opinion, she could only answer, "It's beautiful. But what is it?"

"I recorded it this afternoon. Come here." He took her coffee and placed it with his, then led her by hand up to the alcove and his grand piano. He made himself comfortable on the bench and patted the seat for her to join him. When she did, the temperature of the room rose a few degrees.

He reached for the score he'd been writing the last time. "Remember this?" he asked. She nodded, recognizing the "J" at the top of the sheet. "Well, I finished it. It's for you."

Chapter Eleven

"Me?" Janeen asked, astonished.

"Yes. I wrote it for you. I want to play it for you." Georgios lifted his injured hand and did a few rotating exercises with his thumb. Then, with all the flourish of a seasoned professional, his fingers began to dance along the keys while he closed his eyes as though feeling the music.

Janeen recognized the music she'd just heard on the tape, but this version seemed much more alive. The sounds of the notes weren't entering her ears, they were filtering through every part of her body. Sitting close to him on the bench, she felt his body sway as he reached for the keys, making the mood all the more intense.

She looked up, noticing the floor-length windows open to the warm night air and the curtains billowing in the gentle breeze. Beyond the curtains she saw a full moon watching over a sea of city lights. Without actually seeing it, she knew the sky would be filled with twice as many stars as usual. They would all come out tonight, this very special night.

Adrift in the ambiance, intoxicated by its romance, Janeen thought of the kaleidoscope and all the long hours she'd spent making every detail just right. Now that it was done, she knew it had been a labor of love.

What's more, her career had taken the turn she'd been waiting for all these years. Her scopes would be with a major seller, her name known throughout the world. And she'd done it on her own, with no one's help. All her reasons for keeping Georgios out of her life suddenly vanished. There were no more excuses, nothing but beautiful music, openness, and love.

Ever so softly, Georgios brought a long finger down on the final key, leaving it there as the sound faded into the night. He turned dreamy dark eyes to her but said nothing. She waited. She felt herself drawn into his eyes, like a leaf in a whirlpool.

Without thinking, she wrapped her arms around his neck and brought his lips to meet hers. As she closed her eyes, strong arms enveloped her completely.

After the kiss, Janeen rested her head on Georgios's shoulder. They gazed out at the night in silence, hanging onto the moment before it escaped.

"This is what I've dreamed about since the day I met you," he whispered. "Just you and me and the moonlight."

She looked up at him. "Both our dreams have come true."

His eyes smiled back at her, his passionate gaze enough to drive a woman mad. For all she knew, maybe that's what had happened to her. She had to be mad to stay there with him, like that. Hadn't she sworn not to get involved with him?

Then she remembered how all the obstacles she'd carefully lined up had fallen by the wayside in a few short hours. A contented sigh escaped her smiling lips. She felt like dancing.

"Put on your music," she said.

He sent her an inquisitive glance, then smiled and hurried to the equipment. Within minutes gentle melodic sounds filled the air and she got up to meet him on his return. Falling into his arms, he guided her to the windows where they began to rock and sway to the music. The soft crush of carpeting whispered beneath their feet until she kicked off her shoes and scrunched her toes in the carpet's thickness.

They laughed, they smiled, they danced.

Then what? What would happen to them now? She'd wasted so much time worrying about how to stay away from Georgios. All the years she'd spent suppressing her emotions for the sake of her career hadn't prepared her for what had happened tonight. If she were to be successful, finally, could she also give in to the feeling of love? And was it love, or was she just riding the crest of euphoria, absorbing everything in its wake?

She'd never met anyone who made her feel the way Georgios did. His concern for her was unquestionable. His compassion was undeniable. His sensuality was irresistible.

The music faded and while they waited for the next song, they swayed with the breeze and billowing curtains. The city lights still shone brightly and the moon had risen high in the sky, spreading its glow as far as she could see.

"It's so beautiful up here. I can see why your piano is in this corner. It must be so inspirational when you're writing."

He nodded at the view she'd been admiring. "I don't think I've ever appreciated it as much as I do at this moment." He kissed her ear, sending chills down her arms. "Maybe I'll write a song about it someday."

Was he admitting that he missed his music? "Now that you're writing again, will you get back in the business? You can't deny you love it, it's too much a part of you."

With his mouth at her ear, he whispered, "Yes, I do love it." He squeezed her a little tighter. "But you're a part of me now too." Before he could finish, the alarm on his watch went off. He growled playfully. "I have to go take my medication. Don't move."

He dashed out of the room, which suddenly felt completely empty. She looked around, wondering what time it was, then strode over to the desk area. Their coffee cups blocked a small clock in the corner. As she reached for the clock, she bumped a cup and spilled some coffee. She searched for a tissue, anything to wipe the mess before it rolled to the floor. Opening a drawer she found a discarded napkin, but also noticed a familiar box—from Chatter Box. With a curious sinking awareness, she lifted the lid. Feeling guilty about snooping, but unable to stop, she peeked under the tissue paper.

Janeen stared blankly at her "Seascape" kaleidoscope. *He* had bought it. A strange mixture of emotions rocked her insides until she shook. All at once, everything began to make sense—the missing scopes, the name on the charge slip, Chris's evasiveness, Neiman Marcus.

A sickening feeling took hold of her stomach as reality hit her. It wasn't luck or sheer coincidence that Walter Allen had accepted her proposal. She hadn't even shown him "Seascape." It was Georgios and his meddling, buy-his-way-through-anything way of thinking. Did he think that buying her success was the easiest way to win her over?

A rustle of clothing from behind made her turn. Georgios caught her in his arms, pressing his cheek to hers. Janeen turned out of his hold with a hard shove, then spun around to face him, the taste of venom bitter in her mouth.

"Did you think you could get away with it?"

"Get away with what?"

"Did you think I wouldn't find out?"

"What?" He clenched his jaw tightly.

"I sat there proudly telling you how I'd sold the 'Seascape' while you'd known all along!" She bit into every syllable.

"No, I didn't."

"Don't patronize me. I think I deserve better than that." Her gaze slid to the drawer and the open box.

After following her gaze, he sighed and took a couple of steps toward her, reaching for her arm. "Let me explain."

"Don't touch me," she snapped as she pulled back. "I told you I didn't want help selling my scopes. I warned you to keep your money to yourself. But you went behind my back anyway. Was this all a plan to lure me into your web?"

Calmly, Georgios answered, "I think you should get all the facts before you go making rash statements."

"Rash? You want rash? How about 'Don't you ever interfere in my life again'?"

"I did *not* interfere," he said with gritted teeth.

"And I suppose my kaleidoscope just walked out of my store, over to Neiman Marcus, then ended up in your drawer."

A resigned sigh escaped his lips. "I admit I bought it."

"With Tony's credit card, right? Nice touch." She felt as though she were drowning in a flood of anger against the man who had cunningly deceived her. He tried to reach for her again. "I said not to touch me!"

In frustration, he dropped his hands to his sides. "Will you stop your ranting and listen to me for one minute? I bought the scopes because I thought if I used my influence to open some doors you'd get a head start on marketing them."

"And how much did you have to pay Walter Allen?"

"Nothing!" Annoyed, Georgios sliced the air with his hand. "Can't you get it through your head that all I did was show him the scope? If he decided to buy it, that was strictly his decision. Nor did I know anything about his offer for a new design. The first I heard of it was tonight, from you."

"And where are the other scopes?" She couldn't resist digging for every last detail.

He hesitated a moment, looking as if he were ready to back down. Softly, he answered, "In New York."

"New York! Why?"

"I sent them to a couple of buyers I know."

"Humphh! You are incorrigible." Janeen brushed past him and stormed into the bathroom, slamming the door for effect.

Georgios stared at the closed door, his anger growing more intense every minute that she didn't open it. The woman he loved, the woman that he'd just spent the most wonderful night of his life with, had turned on him. He considered knocking down the door and shaking some sense into her, telling her this was a ridiculous misunderstanding and that he loved her more than any kaleidoscope or musical score.

What did he do that was so terrible? He knew how she hated him using his money for her benefit. But this time he hadn't. He'd only showed the scope to Walter Allen and asked him to consider it.

Nothing he did for her ended up the way he expected. Everything in the last four weeks had been geared toward merging their lives, yet she'd set up more detours than a construction crew. This one had completely thrown him off course.

He didn't know how much more rejection he could take.

All she wanted was to get out of that house and forget about Georgios Andros. He would never understand how important independence was to her. For one short night they'd been like lovers. Now it was back to reality.

She freshened up quickly, determined not to let him see a trace of a tear. Opening the door, she saw him waiting like a pacing tiger. His eyes went from brown to black.

"No matter what you think, I only had your interest in mind," he said in a controlled tone. "In my eyes, there's nothing wrong with helping friends." She tried to skirt around him but he sidestepped and grabbed her wrists. "*Tell* me, what is so wrong with that?"

"Let go of my wrists," she hissed through clenched teeth.

"Not until you tell me why you refuse help."

She glared coldly at him. "I like to be in control of my own life. I don't like anyone else making decisions for me, and I don't accept charity."

She struggled to free her wrists but he held them fast. "Sometimes you need to give in. Sometimes accepting help is a means to an end. It doesn't mean you're any less of a success. It only means you're human, and as human beings we all need help at one time or another."

"If I can't make it on my own, I don't feel it's worth it," she stated flatly.

"But this *was* your own doing. I merely approached a business contact and introduced him to your product. I had no control over him." He relaxed his grip.

"That's exactly what this is all about. Control. You think you can use your money and influence everywhere you go. You wanted to pay me to close the shop early one night. At the Chinese restaurant, you saw to it that we had a private room for as long as we wanted. You even baited me that first day with your big-time deposit."

"And you accepted."

"Yes, because I needed the money."

"And you don't now?"

She finally freed her hands. "No—yes—that's not the point." This whole scene was so frustrating. She couldn't think straight with him standing right in front of her.

"Then explain it to me, help me understand." He'd lowered his voice, but she sensed his frustration hid just below the surface.

Janeen moved around him and back up to the windows to find her shoes. She glanced out for one more quick look. Ironic how beautiful it was outside yet so stormy inside. Maybe he was right. Maybe he deserved an explanation. Something she'd thought was so clear to her might not appear the same to someone else. If you had never had to work for anything in your life, perhaps earning your way would be a completely foreign notion.

He waited near the piano. Taking a deep breath, she began. "To me it's simple. I want my accomplishments to be my own doing, and if I fail I'll have no one to blame but myself."

"But that's just it, you don't have to fail when someone can help you succeed."

"I don't see it that way. For years I've seen my brothers fumble and falter. I watched my father pick them up and set them straight. If they got in trouble, Dad bailed them out."

Puzzled, he asked, "Isn't that natural for a parent?"

"Look at them! One is divorced and chronically unemployed, the other is a lazy, spineless yes-husband. No, I don't think unlimited help is the answer. I'm sick of seeing what they've done to my father. I refuse to do the same."

"Then why is he a part of Chatter Box?"

She was shocked that he knew her closely guarded secret. "What are you talking about? Chatter Box is mine."

"The first day I came into your shop, you were on the phone discussing your father's name in connection with the shop."

Realizing he'd heard more than she'd guessed, she couldn't very well lie. "When I opened the shop, I had no established credit. I needed a cosigner for the lease plus some start-up cash. I've been paying him off faithfully ever since, and as soon as I can renegotiate, I'll get the lease in my name only."

"So you do accept help when necessary," he challenged.

"Look, I don't have to explain any of this to you. I've told you to stay out of my affairs."

"Even if I do it out of love?"

She quickly faced the window. Love? Was he serious? Yes, he was dead serious and she was scared. She'd thought she loved him. She wanted to love him. But she couldn't love a man who would deceive her or go against her principles. She needed someone who was honest, someone who respected her independence.

Close behind her now, his warm breath touched her ear. "Can't you distinguish between interference and love?"

A tremble started somewhere deep inside her. She couldn't stay there any longer without losing a grip on her convictions.

"No more than you can distinguish between your lifelong dream and your desire to walk away from it," she replied flatly as she stepped away. "I have to leave."

He grabbed her shoulders and turned her around to face him. When she looked into his eyes she saw pain, pain for which she knew she was responsible. Softly, she said, "Please, let go of me."

"That's just it," he murmured, "I don't want to let go. I want to be a part of your life. I love you."

She did tremble this time, feeling cold and naked. But her coldness was from within, because she couldn't answer him. He waited, staring hopefully. Finally, as though he'd allotted enough time for her to respond to his profession of love, he abruptly let go. Janeen hurriedly put on her shoes and heard Georgios call Gerald on the intercom.

His tone was flat, completely emotionless when he said, "Miss Warner will be leaving now."

Chapter Twelve

When Georgios finally dragged himself out of bed the next day, he skipped the shower and headed right for the coffee. At the kitchen table, Tony barely looked up from the paper.

"I know I must be in the obituaries today because that woman killed me last night." Tony didn't respond. "She cut me open, ripped my heart out, and threw it in the blender." He plopped down, spilling his coffee, and snarled at the mess.

Tony folded the paper and slid a plate of muffins across the table. Georgios shoved them back. "Not hungry."

"You're not supposed to take your medication on an empty stomach," Tony reminded him.

Georgios grumbled, grabbed his pill bottle, and took a capsule with a long gulp of coffee.

"Why don't you at least have milk to coat your stomach."

"I don't want anything," he roared. "And I don't care if it bothers my stomach because I couldn't possibly feel any worse than I already do. I feel like I've been beaten up." He paused as an idea hit him. "That workout room you and Gerald use downstairs, you got a punching bag in there?"

Tony hesitantly answered. "Yes."

Georgios slammed his fist down on the table rattling the cups. "That's what I want to do. Punish the bag. Come on."

He led the way down, Tony a reluctant follower. "Sir, you've never done this before and I don't think it's a good idea with your hand still healing."

"Then tape me up and strap on those gloves over there."

As soon as the gloves were fastened, Georgios started punching the bag. Tony stepped to the back and held it steady. It felt good to hit something. It felt good to get his anger out. But he needed more. He needed to get all the emotion out of his system.

"She insulted me, Tony. She rejected my love and she walked out." He pummeled the bag in rapid succession. "I always knew that when I fell in love, I'd fall hard. I never expected it to be this painful though. I'm successful and rich, yet the one woman I fall in love with despises my fame and fortune." He slammed his fist into the bag and grimaced at the pain.

"I don't think that's an accurate assessment."

"What do you mean? I've tried to help her, but she says she'd rather struggle on her own without help."

Tony held the bag firm against a flurry of hits. Quietly, in his deep monotone voice, he said, "How would you feel if you were trying desperately to write a song and someone came along and said 'Let me do it for you'? Or, if you couldn't play again—which almost wasn't too far from the truth—and someone said they'd play for you? Isn't that like stealing your thunder?"

Georgios stopped. His head was beginning to pound and he felt a little dizzy. Maybe Tony was right, not eating wasn't such a good idea. But he liked pounding the bag and he liked how this bonding helped loosen Tony's usually quiet tongue.

"So you think I should just butt out, leave her alone?"

"As far as what's between the two of you, I can't offer any advice. As for her career, yes. Butt out. Let her make her mistakes or her achievements. She's a proud woman."

Georgios walked to the bench set for a towel. Sweat had beaded on his forehead. He wiped it quickly, then shook off the dizziness before returning to the bag. Round two.

"You're right," he grumbled. "Stay out of her business. But what about our relationship? How do I get her back?"

Tony took the force of more blows behind the bag without flinching. "Like I said, I can't give you any advice in that area, but I can tell you what you should do for yourself."

"What? Take a vacation?"

"Harness this anger and frustration and focus it. There's a lot of raw emotion surfacing, feelings that have been under wraps for a long time. Use it. Play it. Turn it into music."

"What good would it do? It wouldn't make any difference to Janeen if I were famous or disappeared into oblivion." He stopped punching and labored for air. His vision grew dim. "My music is about love," Georgios scoffed. "How can I write about love when I don't even know what it is?" He slammed a hard punch into the bag.

Tony stepped aside, the bag swung out and right back into an unprepared Georgios. He went down like a crumpled piece of paper. "Just give it a try, Georgios," Tony said from above. "You might be surprised at what happens."

Georgios blinked away stars. He took some deep breaths, waiting for the feeling to return to his nose. He heard Tony inquiring if he was okay, but he was more preoccupied with letting what Tony had said sink in. Slowly his pulse returned to normal and the room stopped spinning. His music. Could that be the answer? Was Tony right, should he give it a try?

Then something else struck him, harder than the bag had. "Did you just call me Georgios?"

"No, sir."

"Yes you did, I heard you. You called me by my name."

Tony lent a hand to help his employer up. "Let's get you in the shower. You're punch-drunk."

Before her Tuesday meeting at Neiman Marcus, Janeen was a pacing bundle of nerves. But then, she'd been that way since she left Georgios on Saturday. For three days, whenever the phone rang she half-expected, half-hoped it would be him, then berated herself when it wasn't. His admission of love burned deep in her memory but it did nothing to change her

anger at his deception. And she still couldn't accept
Walter Allen's offer.

The phone rang as she was about to leave the store
for her appointment. "Chatter Box, may I help you?"

"Hi, honey."

"Hi, Dad," she answered glumly.

"Now there's a welcome if I ever heard one."

"Sorry, I was just on my way out."

"I won't keep you long." He spoke in a low voice.
"I just received a call from the management group.
They're looking for the rent."

Janeen couldn't believe she was late again. It
seemed like she'd just made a payment, now another
one was due. Had it really been over a month since
Georgios had come to the rescue?

"I've told them over and over you have nothing to
do with the business." Would she now be a failure in
her father's eyes?

"Janeen, my name is on the lease. Of course they're
going to contact me when payments are delinquent. I
can make the payment this month if you need a little
breather."

"No! I can handle it. What is it with you men and
your need to take over?"

"*You men?* Are you talking about George? If he
tried to help, it's only because he cares about you."

"Did he call you?" she asked suspiciously.

"No. I just know from our conversations that he's
concerned about your business and would be willing
to help in any way he could. I also know you and how
stubborn you can be."

"Well, we know what side of the family that comes
from."

"That's right, and as your stubborn father I have the

right to tell you you're wrong. Everyone needs a little help at some time in their life. It's nothing to be ashamed of, and if it comes from someone who loves you, you're doing them a favor by accepting. Think about everything you could lose for the sake of a little pride. Is it worth it?"

Silent, because all the fight had gone out of her, Janeen knew what he said made sense. Yet it was so opposite from what she believed, regardless of how much she loved him. Now was not the time to try to make sense out of her confused emotions.

"Dad, I have to go. I have an appointment. Don't worry about the payment. I . . . I have some money coming." If she got up the nerve to collect it, that is.

"Okay, but remember, I'm always here."

"Come in, Ms. Warner." Walter Allen held the door open.

Janeen smiled as she entered the Neiman Marcus purchasing agent's office in Copley Plaza. She took a seat in front of his unkempt desk strewn with brochures, folders, and coffee cups.

"You'll have to excuse the mess," he began. "I'm in the middle of buying for the Christmas season." From a mountainous pile in front of him he pulled out a folder with the large black letters "Oriental Collection" written across the top. "I'd like you to take a look at some of the designs in here. This is the look we want for our fall collection."

Taken by surprise with his down-to-business approach, Janeen put down her leather bag and flipped through the designs.

"As you can see, we're planning a full array of household items and gifts. I think a kaleidoscope would fit in nicely with our more affluent clientele. Do you foresee any problem achieving an Oriental look in a kaleidoscope?"

"Not at all. There are a number of possibilities." Even as she spoke, a barrage of images swam around in her head. She pictured bamboo encasements, porcelain wheels, colored rice. An exciting project. Just what she needed.

"Good. Can you have something for photography by the first of July?"

Obviously Walter Allen was a no-nonsense kind of man. His discarded jacket hung on the back of his chair. His tie was loose, his sleeves were rolled up, and he'd smoothly swept her into the world of big-time merchandising as though they'd been working together for years. He had confidence in her.

"Certainly," Janeen asserted, giddy with her own confidence in herself and her ability.

"Okay," he continued, "that settles the new design. Now, what about the. . . ." He checked some notes on a desk pad, looking for something he'd obviously written as a reminder. His finger stopped on the page. " 'Seascape.' How soon can we get some?"

Janeen's earlier ease suddenly vanished. She thought about her discovery of the scope in Georgios's drawer and how betrayed she'd felt. Even worse, there seemed to be no explanation to make him understand what he'd done. As she replayed the ugly scene in her head, all the anger and frustration came rushing back. She gripped the arms of her chair tighter. No matter what the consequences, she could not bring herself to let Georgios's intervention be a deciding factor in her career.

"Ms. Warner?" Walter Allen questioned her distraction.

"I'm sorry. I have a bit of a problem with that."

"What kind of problem? I thought you said you had them in stock." He dropped his glasses on top of his desk.

"I do, but I don't think I can sell them to you." She heard the words come out of her mouth, but she couldn't believe she'd actually said them. She was refusing a sale.

"Is this some kind of joke?"

Janeen swallowed hard. Her hands were sweaty. She wished she had a glass of water. "No, I'm afraid it isn't." There was no backing down now. She had to explain herself.

"I know that the only reason you want to buy the 'Seascape' is because of Georgios Andros. I don't know what he told you or how he persuaded you, but I'm well aware of his powerful influence. Unfortunately, I can't allow it to be a deciding factor in how I run my business. I apologize if this makes me look ungrateful, but I have some strong principles."

She watched Walter Allen lean back in his chair, touching a finger to his lips. She'd probably blown the whole deal with Neiman Marcus. Who knew? She might even be blackballed from all department stores in the entire United States forever.

"I'd still be happy to work with you on the Oriental line," she continued. "Assuming Mr. Andros had nothing to do with it."

Walter Allen sat forward, resting his forearms on the edge of his desk. "You are the first person I've ever had sit in that chair and decline an offer to buy.

Neiman Marcus has a reputation for quality products. I didn't get to this position by kissing up or playing favorites."

Janeen's knees began to shake. The room suddenly seemed dark and overbearing, as though a cloud had filled it like an ominous monster. She felt dizzy at the prospect of losing the best deal that had ever come her way.

Putting his glasses on, Walter Allen peered at the list on his desk again. "Yes, Georgios Andros visited me. He's one of our VIP clients." His tone was clear and concise, edged with irritation. "He gets preferential treatment when it comes to shopping and ordering. That's where it ends. I make decisions based on my experience and my ability, not because someone directs or persuades me in any way."

He took a sip of coffee from a half-filled cup. "I promised Georgios nothing. I told him I would consider the kaleidoscope and he left. I called you because *I* decided the 'Seascape' was what I wanted. The scope sold itself. Nothing else." She heard the how-dare-you-think-otherwise implication.

Janeen hung her head and looked at her hands, afraid she'd offended him. Could it be? Had she really won this account on her own ability? Had her dream finally come true? A lightness lifted her heart, knowing his interference hadn't been the deal breaker.

"I apologize for sounding so righteous, but it is very important to me to be taken seriously."

And that was the final sticking question. Did Georgios take her seriously or had his intervention been a ploy to win her over? She didn't really believe that, but now was not the time to ponder it to death. With business at hand, she looked up when Walter Allen stood.

"My offer is still open. I hope you'll reconsider your decision. But if you don't, there are a hundred other vendors waiting to step into the vacancy." He approached her chair, a signal that the meeting was over. Holding the door open, he said, "You have a great talent, Ms. Warner. Don't let it go to waste."

Janeen pored over her bills. Everything that was due, including the rent, left her eight hundred dollars short. Sales had been brisk all week, but there was no way to know from one day to the next. With a sigh, she decided to take a chance and write out checks for everything except her salary. If sales over the next few days didn't live up to expectations, she'd have to survive on peanut butter and crackers and suffer the consequences of an overdraft.

By Friday, the store took in only six hundred. Janeen's hopes of a deposit big enough to cover the checks dwindled. Try as she might, she could think of only one way to get a lump sum—a solution she'd been stubbornly avoiding.

She had to get the money Georgios owed her for the kaleidoscope.

But how could she put a price on the project she'd done for him? It had been a labor of love. No amount of money equaled what had gone into it. But she knew she had no choice. She'd already called Walter Allen, after his convincing speech that Georgios had no influence on his decision, and agreed to sell him her 'Seascapes.' That, plus the new Oriental design, meant she needed supplies to get started. Supplies cost money. She had no money.

Frantically searching her leather bag, she finally found Georgios's card at the bottom. So much had happened since she'd first held that card. Their relationship had escalated in a way she'd never thought possible. Calling him now would be the closest she'd ever come to begging. But what choice did she have? They had made a business deal, she'd produced, now he owed. Simple.

Far from it, she thought as she shakily dialed the number. When she got his answering machine, she was almost relieved for an easy way out. Yet Janeen didn't feel any relief when she hung up. She'd quickly relayed her reason for calling and asked that he remit the amount due as quickly as possible. She'd half-expected him to pick up, but he hadn't. Nor did he return her call that night, the next day, or the next week.

Somehow, she made it through her financial crisis without any more collection calls and only one check bouncing. Pleasant weather rolled in the following week bringing with it increased consumer traffic and comfortable sales. She also received payment for the three scopes delivered to Neiman Marcus. Things were definitely looking up.

Then why didn't she feel any better?

Four weeks had passed since she'd walked out on Georgios. June was in bloom in the city. Tourists were pouring into the shop daily, laying down their money. Early one quiet morning, she sat on her stool behind the counter, sipping a coffee while reviewing the week's intake. She saw the long legs coming down the stairs before she actually heard their steps, but in her daze she dismissed them as fantasy. A pleasant memory of a cool day in April flashed through her mind.

Her reverie came to an abrupt halt as the buzzer sounded and the shadow of a tall man loomed over her. "Tony! What are you doing here?" Janeen jumped off her stool and peeked around the hulking man to peer out the door. There, outside, stood Georgios, leaning patiently against the cement wall that formed the stairwell. "And what is *he* doing out there? Aren't things a little backwards? You're supposed to be protecting him."

"He thought it was safer this way. For him, there's more danger in here than out there."

She couldn't help but smile at the twist and she didn't blame him for his concern. "I see his point." Even in the shadow of the stairs, she could tell he was casually dressed in jeans and a white T-shirt with a shoe logo across the front. She felt a familiar stirring somewhere deep inside. The casual look was a marked change from when they first met.

Although she'd been looking around the large, formidable figure of Tony, she noticed how he was nervously shifting from one foot to the other. He was too used to being the one in the shadows, not the one in the front doing the talking.

"What can I do for you, Tony?"

He cleared his throat. "Mr. Andros wanted you to have this right away." He handed her an envelope. "He's been away and he just got your message. He sends his apologies for the delay."

Janeen lifted the flap of the envelope. The check inside stirred a strange mixture of emotions in her. She was relieved to have the scope payment, but at the same time it marked the end of something. There would no longer be any reason for them to pretend a relationship, business or otherwise.

"Tell Mr. Andros thank you." She sniffed away a telltale tear. "It was a pleasure doing business with him."

Tony sent her a knowing look. The look said he knew it had been more pleasure than business and she was foolish for pretending it hadn't. Then his look changed to determination.

"Mr. Andros has something else for you, but I think it should come from him." Tony turned and walked out the door.

She watched the lively interaction between the two men outside. Tony took something out of his suit coat and pushed it into Georgios's hand. Georgios seemed reluctant, but Tony insisted. With a quick tug, Tony pulled Georgios away from the wall, exchanged places with him and pushed his employer toward the door. Georgios stood at the door for a long, unnerving moment. Janeen tried to prepare herself for their awkward meeting, but all she could do was hold her breath and hope that her voice didn't shake as much as her knees were.

When he finally entered, he slowly approached the counter and smiled apprehensively. "Hi."

"Hi." His dark eyes looked sad. His handsome face seemed thin. She hated to think she had a part in his tired look but the sadness in his eyes told her she was guilty. "How are you?"

"Good. A little tired, but good. I've been in New York for the past month. Working."

"Working?"

"Yes. I finished my CD." He lifted his hand and

offered her a cassette. "This is a demo. I'd like you to have it."

She placed the check on the counter and took the unmarked cassette. "Thanks. I look forward to listening to it."

Her gaze drifted downward to his hand on the counter. The scar was dark purple, but smoothly healed. "How's the hand?"

"Great." He made a full circle with his thumb. "Almost as good as new." With one finger, he tipped her chin up and gazed deeply into her eyes. "Some things heal faster than others."

She knew what that meant. She'd hurt him deeply. But did he understand her reasons for leaving?

He quickly grabbed her hands, as though afraid she would run away. A gasp caught in her throat.

"I want you to listen to this with your heart," he said, squeezing her fingers around the plastic case. One corner dug into her palm. She looked into his eyes, which now shone with a new light. "This album is very special to me. I want it to be special to you. You will be the first person, outside of my manager and studio technicians, to hear it."

Unable to answer, she nodded, afraid to look away.

He released the tight hold on her hands, but gently held on to her fingers. "How have you been?" he whispered. "You look . . . as good as ever. Maybe better."

"I've been very busy. Tourist season is here and I'm working on the designs for Neiman Marcus."

She thought she saw relief wash across his face. "That's great. I was afraid you'd turn down Walter Allen's offer."

"I did, actually. But he's a great guy. He made me realize it wasn't worth losing out on a lifelong dream because of a little foolish pride." She pulled her hands out of his and placed the tape on the counter.

"So you believe me that I was only doing it for your benefit?" he asked in a hopeful tone.

"Oh, I believe you. I've always believed that what you were doing was for my benefit. What I don't think you've ever understood is that I didn't want you to do anything. I didn't want your money or your influence playing any kind of role in my career. I will make my own way. I have to do it on my own."

Georgios reached for the check on the counter. "So, you don't want this either, right?"

Janeen slapped her hand down on the payment she'd been waiting for. "That's different. That was a business deal."

"Why is it different than my helping your career along?"

"Call me stubborn, call me stupid, call me whatever you want. We had a contract. I made you a kaleidoscope, you paid me for it. That's it, it's over."

Georgios inched his way around the counter until he was barely a breath away. "What's over? The deal, or us?"

Dangerously passionate eyes burned into her. She didn't know how much longer she could resist their draw. "The deal."

"But not us?"

"I . . . don't know." Her words came out staggered. Her thoughts jumped all around. "I can't think about that right now. I have too much to do."

"You always say that. Your life is a constant string of too much to do. But I'm living proof that you can drop it all without the world coming to an end. Believe me, when you pick it up again, it's like you were never gone."

"Maybe for you, but it's different for me."

"And why is it different for you? What sets you apart from everyone else?" His words were biting, but his voice was soft. He'd placed his hands on her arms, making her feel so much smaller beneath his penetrating gaze.

"It's not what sets me apart from everyone else, it's what sets *you* apart. You're famous. You're rich. You can do anything you want and your adoring public will still be there. Me, I'm nobody. If I want to keep my place on the road to success, I have to stay on track. If I drop out of line, the next person will just move up to take my place."

"Hmmm. Sounds like a well-prepared speech."

"It should be. I've said it enough to my family."

He slid his hands to her shoulders, then up to cradle her face. "If I told you that success can be a lonely place when there's no one to share it with, would it make a difference?"

Janeen swallowed hard. Tears stung her eyes. She knew about loneliness and what it felt like when everyday achievements and highlights went unnoticed by anyone special. She had no one to come home to, no one to share her trials and tribulations with. It hadn't really mattered that much to her, until she met Georgios.

"I'm sure that's true, but I won't stop trying."

She'd managed to answer without tears spilling over. But her traitorous eyes shifted to his lips and before she knew it, he was kissing her. His soft mouth pressed gently on her quivering lips. She couldn't help but respond, wrapping her arms around his neck. Their kiss was long and meaningful.

He finally lifted his mouth and murmured, "Neither will I." He gave her a quick kiss on the cheek. "You are what I've wanted all my life. I want to be there when you reach your goal, to celebrate with you. I want to be a part of your happiness and I want you to be a part of mine."

She rested her cheek on his chest. His heart beat soundly, comfortingly. "You make it sound so easy."

"It is easy. Just say yes."

"No. It's not easy." She lifted her head and backed up a step, gaining strength as she gained distance. "I have to work hard at it. I don't lead a charmed life."

Like you, she wanted to say. She continued to pull away from his hold. "This project with Neiman Marcus requires all my concentration. What's left of my time is devoted to this shop. It's what pays the bills for the time being."

He caught her fingertips. "I don't like it, but I admire your determination. When you make a decision, you stick to it."

Janeen let out a sigh, relieved they weren't fighting. He understood. "What about you? Why the change of heart, going back to the music?"

"You. You made me realize I couldn't give up something I've worked for all my life. You gave me back my music."

Janeen looked down, embarrassed that he credited her with his achievement. "Oh, I'm sure you would have found your music, with or without me."

He gave a little laugh and touched the back of his finger to her cheek. "You have no idea what a difference you've made in my life, do you? Oddly enough, this CD wouldn't have been possible without you—or with you for that matter."

She looked questioningly at him. "That doesn't make sense."

"I know. But it all made sense in the studio. I hope you'll like the results." He lifted her hand to his lips and sensuously kissed her palm before placing the demo tape in it.

Then he was gone.

Chapter Thirteen

That night Janeen listened to the tape. As always, she fell under his musical spell. Each song, each note, spoke to her intimately. She could feel all the emotions he'd felt when he wrote and played the music. Sitting in her dark living room, she let each song take hold of her and wrap her in its warmth.

The final song struck a familiar chord. It was "J," the song he'd written and played for her their last night together. Tears filled her eyes as she remembered the billowing curtains, his piano, his beautiful music room. So much had happened to them since then, almost as if they had been two other people. Could she have been in love? Had she thrown it all away?

He'd seemed so sure of himself during their weeks together, yet today he acted differently, subdued, as though something had changed. Yes, he'd gone back to his music, but had he given up on love? Did the new CD mean he was hungry for fame again or that he had resolved his conflicts as to why he wrote music?

Janeen groaned. Maybe the change wasn't in him, but her.

The song ended with loud, reverberating bass drums and she burst into uncontrollable tears.

Janeen delivered the final version of "Moonrise" to Walter Allen and felt a satisfaction like nothing she'd ever experienced since her graduation from college. It had been a flawless project and he was very pleased with her design.

"I think we've got a winner with this item," he said. "It should be a big hit at the show."

"Show?" She had no idea what he was talking about.

"Yes. We're having a special opening in two weeks to introduce the Oriental line and premiere our gift selections for the holiday season. Buyers from all over the country will be there. I've arranged a special designer's display for your scopes and you'll be there as the woman behind the design."

She left his office in a daze. Her designs were to be on display in Neiman Marcus and featured in an exclusive showing! Was this the moment that would change everything?

Deep down she knew she'd already changed, the night she'd cried herself to sleep after listening to Georgios's tape. His music had softened her heart, knowing it was meant for no one but her and him. The love he'd poured out on that little tape had grabbed her and shaken her into believing that maybe they did have a chance. Maybe it wasn't too late for her to let go and let love into her life—after the Neiman Marcus show.

A few days later her invitation arrived—formal attire required. She'd never attended a formal occasion in her life and she certainly had nothing formal to wear.

Her first instinct was to excuse herself from attending, but that would be the cowardly way out. If she was to be a success, she had to act the part. She needed to find a way to buy an outfit suitable for a successful, established designer.

"Hi, Dad." After much thought and an enormous amount of soul-searching, she'd decided to ask her father for help. "Would it be possible to have a short-term loan? I can pay you back in a couple of weeks, but I need a lump sum right away."

"Who is this?" Howard Warner pretended shock.

"Very funny, Dad."

"Is this Janeen? My daughter? The one who never accepts a dime from anyone?"

"Dad, this is serious." She explained her need and how her credit card was nearly maxed out. "So, could you swing a loan?"

"Sure, why not? It doesn't look like I'll be paying for a wedding dress anytime soon."

She spent the next week checking out all the boutiques in and around Faneuil Hall in her spare time, but without much success. Determined to find the perfect dress for her "coming out", she took a ride to Newbury Street. After the third store, the sticker shock finally wore off enough for her to actually try on some dresses. At the last shop, she fell in love with a royal blue gown. Slightly off the shoulder and with a Vneck bodice, the fitted dress accented her shape perfectly. Janeen held her breath as she turned in front of the three-way mirror.

"You look like a song," said the saleswoman.

Janeen tilted her head at the woman. What an odd thing for her to say.

Copley Plaza buzzed with excitement the night of the show. Taxis and limousines lined the street in front of Neiman Marcus as invited guests arrived for the exclusive event. Security checked each guest off a list and presented them with a tiny gold umbrella pin that had to be worn to gain admission.

The crowd was still small, but growing every minute. Janeen quickly found Walter Allen, who graciously introduced her to some coworkers before escorting her to the giftware displays. Front and center, her designated place of honor was more than she could have hoped for. A surge of pride swelled in her chest as she stood in front of the beige and black background painted with bamboo huts and rice paddies. Her "Moonrise" kaleidoscope sat on a black cradle atop a raised red platform. It looked like a precious gem on exhibit.

"Well, what do you think?" Walter asked.

Tears stung her eyes while an emotional lump caught in her throat. She had waited for this day for so long. "It's beautiful. Thank you, Walter."

"Don't thank me. You did it."

"But if it weren't for you believing in me and ignoring my stupid ramblings, I wouldn't even be standing here."

"Show me a successful person and I'll show you a

list of people he or she credits with helping them get there. No one does it alone. Be thankful for *all* those who believe in you."

She spent the next few hours greeting observers and answering questions as people looked into the scope. Waiters worked their way through the guests with silver platters of hors d'oeuvres and champagne. Janeen marveled at the posh, ritzy atmosphere of men in tuxedos and women in evening gowns and jewels. She felt as though she'd been transported into another world.

"Ms. Warner?"

Janeen turned to face the woman who had just set the scope back on its cradle. "Yes?"

"I'm Lauren Siegel. I'm a buyer with Werner Dresser."

Janeen's mouth nearly dropped open. She recognized the name as one of the most prestigious department stores in New York City. After presenting her card, the woman continued.

"I tried calling you this afternoon. Your delightful assistant—Chris, is it?—said you'd taken the afternoon off. I was hoping we could connect while I was in town. I didn't realize you'd be here tonight, but now I see why." She nodded approvingly toward the kaleidoscope.

Janeen couldn't imagine why this woman wanted to see her or how she knew of her store.

"Georgios Andros left one of your kaleidoscopes with me a few months ago." Click. The wheels began to turn. Janeen remembered Georgios sheepishly admitting he'd sent the other two scopes to New York. "I've been meaning to call you but with the buying season so crazy, I never got around to it."

The old feelings of resentment began to surface as she glanced at the business card. With a great deal of effort, she forced herself to remember she wasn't angry at Georgios anymore. "What can I do for you, Ms. Siegel?"

"I'd like to purchase a few scopes for our store. I loved the 'Fantasia' right off, but I had to bring it to committee, which took some time. In the end, the general consensus was buy it. Would you be able to send some out before September?"

The sudden realization of what she said hit Janeen like a boulder. Her scope had been approved by a committee of people who liked it for what it was, not because Georgios forced it upon them. It tasted like success. It tasted like validation. She smiled from ear to ear.

"Of course." They closed the deal with a handshake and Lauren Siegel's promise to call when she got back to New York.

As the time crept past 10:00, Janeen wondered how long she was expected to stay. The crowd hadn't thinned at all; in fact, it seemed to have grown. Stifling a yawn, she thought she saw a flash near the entrance. A growing murmur and a rippling of people flowed into the room. She noticed a throng of onlookers jockeying for position as someone of obvious celebrity made their way in. Suddenly the room exploded with flashes.

She watched curiously as photographers snapped picture after picture, cameras held high. A few reporters edged in closer, their microphones thrust forward in an almost comical hubbub. As the group got closer, she recognized two familiar heads standing tall above the crowd. Tony and Georgios.

His attendance didn't really surprise her, but somehow she'd put the possibility out of her head. She'd been too busy concentrating on making a good impression.

But Georgios's grand entrance, and all the commotion it caused, momentarily threw her. Except for the autograph seekers in the Market, their time together had always been private. She now realized how precious his visits to her apartment or her parents' house must have been to him. He'd been able to relax without crowds or reporters hounding him. He'd been himself.

It hadn't occurred to her that being famous also meant constantly being watched. It meant putting on a public face.

Something in her feelings for Georgios crystallized at that moment, like an image brought into focus in one of her scopes. Though the image could change with a turn of the cylinder, what was inside remained constant.

What they'd shared over the past few months was special only to them; no one could add to or detract from it. Seeing the crowd around him, all wanting a piece of the famous Georgios Andros, she wanted to jump in and protect him, save him from the savages. She wanted to cradle him in her arms where no one could touch him. She wanted him for herself.

She loved him.

No sooner had she admitted that inner feeling than the crowd split open. Tony led the way and stood before Janeen's display facing the crowd, while Georgios inched forward. Cameras rolled, lights flashed, but for one moment while they gazed into each other's eyes, it was only Janeen and Georgios, alone.

He looked magnificent in a black tux, his dark handsome features offset by the white shirt. His eyes sparkled like deep dark pools of starlight. The straight line of his lips turned up slightly at the corners as he stared at Janeen.

At long last, he looked down at the 'Moonrise' scope and tilted his head ever so slightly. "May I?"

She wasn't sure if she said yes, nodded, or gestured, but he picked up the scope and peered through the lens. As he turned the chamber, her mind's eye shared what he saw. A moment later, he handed the scope to her, letting his fingers linger and brand her skin with his undeniable heat.

"Beautiful," he whispered. The crowd buzzed, more lights flashed, then he was swallowed up and swept away by Tony.

Janeen felt herself being swallowed up too—by loneliness. She wanted him to take her into his strong arms and kiss her until there wasn't a breath left in her chest. She wanted to tell him she loved him. But he was gone. Gone with the public who adored him. How could she possibly compete?

"Excuse me, Ms. Warner?"

Startled that someone still remained, Janeen blinked at the local reporter, a tall woman with a notepad in hand. She'd apparently decided there might be a story here, not with the moving crowd.

"What was that all about? Are you and Georgios an item?"

Janeen's face grew warm. "No, we're just . . . acquainted."

"Is this why he called his new CD 'Kaleidoscope'?"

"What?" Her back stiffened. "Did you say 'Kaleidoscope'?"

"Yes. That's the CD he's promoting tonight. Didn't you know?" Janeen shook her head, dumbfounded. "He's performing at midnight, according to the program."

The reporter handed her the program. Apparently satisfied she'd learned all she could from Janeen, the woman left to rejoin the competition. Janeen scanned the program.

A midnight concert at the Waterfall Atrium in the Plaza. Georgios Andros performs from his upcoming CD, Kaleidoscope.

Her head swam. The title astounded her. Why hadn't he told her? She guessed the answer was in the music itself. The old Janeen would have thought this was his way of manipulating her again. The new Janeen understood what was in his heart when she'd listened to the tape. She'd seen his soul.

I have to talk to him.

Working her way through the crowd, she went to the door that opened onto the plaza. A security guard reminded her she needed her umbrella pin if she wanted to come back in. "Did you see which way Georgios Andros went?" she asked the man.

"I believe he headed for the atrium, but I doubt if you'll get near him."

He was probably right. The guests inside Neiman Marcus were there by invitation, while the plaza was open to the public. By now, Tony would have ushered Georgios to a secure place, away from the crowd in the plaza.

Uncertain, she lingered in the doorway, until a hand on her shoulder made her turn. "Gerald! Oh, I'm so glad to see you. Is there any way I can talk to Georgios? It's very important."

She thought she saw him fight back a smile. "He's gone to check the equipment on the stage and get ready for the concert."

"Please, Gerald. I need to see him."

This time he did smile. "I'll see what I can do."

She watched the driver make his way through the busy plaza and disappear near the center. Not one for patience, she tapped her foot and fidgeted with her gold umbrella pin while preparing herself for disappointment. Georgios had a job to do. There were too many people around. There wasn't time for small talk. Security needed to be tight.

Ten minutes later, Gerald returned, out of breath from hurrying. "Come with me. Quickly."

He took her arm and they nearly ran toward the atrium. Gerald escorted her behind the huge waterfall that dropped from the sky lobby two stories up. Barriers formed a makeshift dressing room across from the elevators and Tony stood guard at the entrance. Tony nodded for her to enter and moved the curtain aside. Her heart pounded as loudly as the sound of the waterfall on the marble floor.

When she entered, she saw Georgios in a chair being fussed over by a woman with a makeup sponge. His jacket had been removed and his open shirt collar—lined with tissue—exposed that dark thatch of hair Janeen loved so much.

He beamed when he caught sight of her. "Come in. Sorry I wasn't more hospitable at your display, but with the press breathing down my neck I thought it inappropriate."

"I understand." She hadn't at the time, but she now realized how calculated all his public moves had to be.

"Gerald said you wanted to talk to me."

Janeen glanced at the makeup lady. She assumed the woman would either leave on her own or Georgios would dismiss her, but she never stopped her sponging. Janeen found it impossible to gather her thoughts while he sat there having his face dabbed.

She hedged forward. "I just wanted to thank you."

"Thank me. For what?"

"For everything you've done. I know I seemed ungrateful, but I do appreciate all the trouble you took. Lauren Siegel approached me tonight. She wants to take on the 'Fantasia.' "

"That's great. I'm very happy for you."

"I feel like I owe everything to you."

"That isn't true. It was your talent that got you here. I only opened a few doors."

"I know that now. I just wish I hadn't been so stubborn in coming to that realization."

Tony poked his head around the curtain. "They're ready for the sound check, sir."

Janeen's pulse picked up. She still hadn't told him she loved him. She looked at the woman who now applied blush to Georgios's cheeks with quick strokes of a large brush. Janeen wanted to throw the brush in the air and jump into his arms.

But as the thought passed through her mind, he rose from the chair, pulling the tissue out of his collar. With a crooked smile, he went to Janeen and placed his hands on her shoulders.

"And I have you to thank for this night. You helped me get my life into focus. If it weren't for you, I might never have done this." He lowered his voice and spoke close to her ear. "See how we complement each other? We've exchanged talents. I gave you your scopes and you gave me my music."

Janeen closed her eyes, waiting to join him in a kiss. Instead, he slid his hands from her shoulders and exited through the curtain. For a moment, she thought he would come back in after giving an order to someone.

But he didn't. She heard the sounds of violins tuning up, keyboards being tapped, and horns tested. Someone at a microphone repeated, "Testing, one, two, testing, testing, one, two," until she wanted to scream.

With one last glance back at the makeup woman who was packing away the cosmetics, Janeen dashed out of the curtained area and into the crowd. People were lining up everywhere—around the atrium on all three levels of the plaza, along the walkways, on the temporarily halted escalator. Everyone waited for the show. Everyone wanted a piece of Georgios. Everyone.

She looked up at the shimmering curtains that hid the stage from the audience and felt as though a curtain had also been hung between her and Georgios. He had an audience again and his job was to please them. Where did that leave her? Always behind a curtain? Why had it taken her so long to realize what he meant to her?

Tears threatened to spill from her eyes. With no tissue at hand, she turned to find a restroom. A gentle hand tugged her forearm, holding her back. Smiling sympathetically, Gerald held out a clean, white handkerchief. She accepted it gratefully and dabbed the corners of her eyes while walking to a nearby wall. She leaned against one of Gucci's display windows.

"I guess I look pretty silly, huh?"

"Not at all." Gerald politely looked away.

"Well, I seem to be the only one in the crowd crying."

"You also were the only one who talked to him before the show."

Janeen studied Gerald, trying to read his meaning. But his face had closed up and he'd quickly resumed the role of faithful, subservient employee. She finished wiping her moist eyes and folded up the hanky.

Just then, all the lights in the plaza dimmed and the crowd came alive with oohs, aahs, and cheers. A voice came over the sound system. "Ladies and gentlemen! Neiman Marcus, in conjunction with Copley Plaza, is proud to present Boston's very own, Georgios Andros!"

A drum announced itself loudly, then a violin cried out. More violins joined in, picking up the tempo, while bass fiddles added rhythm. The drums split the air with thunderous rumbles and the circular curtain fell to the floor accompanied by loud applause from the audience.

Janeen found herself drawn to the center by the power of the music. She had listened to Georgios's tapes, but hearing him live with his orchestra was a more passionate experience than she could have dreamed. The music was compelling, vibrant. It shook the floor beneath her feet and worked its way up to awaken the butterflies in her stomach.

Once again Gerald was at her side, moving her forward until they came to the cordoned off area behind the waterfall. A security guard opened the barrier and Gerald prompted her toward the stage. They stopped when they reached Tony. He nodded to Gerald, as though exchanging a signal, and pulled Janeen by the hand to stand beside him.

Bright lights shone from every direction around the octagon-shaped Atrium. Musicians crowded the seemingly small stage that had been erected on the marble floor in front of the waterfall. In the middle of it all stood Georgios with three keyboards set up in a U-shape. He moved from one to another, fingers skittering over keys as their lovely sounds filled the air. He looked magnificent, glorious, happy. Then, as though he knew she was there, he raised his eyes from the keys, looked straight at her, and smiled radiantly.

Her heart melted.

The song continued until the sudden dramatic close of horns and drums. Georgios threw his arms up and the crowd roared.

Taking a microphone, he bowed. "Thank you, thank you. It's a pleasure to be here tonight. After almost two years, I've just completed a new CD and the selections you will hear tonight are from it." A loud round of applause echoed through the plaza.

"A special person in my life once said that I used money to buy anything I wanted. That may have been true, but I've learned and I've changed. All the proceeds from this CD will be going to a special fund set up for the homeless in the Boston area." Another round of applause cheered him on.

"I've called the CD 'Kaleidoscope' because I met a woman who makes the most beautiful kaleidoscopes. Her creations inspired my music more than anything I've ever experienced. She is very special to me and I've written a song for her—'Janeen.' "

Georgios put down the microphone and the crowd applauded, waiting for the music to begin. Janeen held her breath as she watched him walk toward her. *This can't be happening.* He took her hand and pulled her to the center of the stage. The audience cheered and whistled while Georgios led her to the piano bench and placed her like a princess on a throne.

"What are you doing?" she whispered.

"Making love to you," he answered.

He sat down next to her and began the song she now knew by heart. The pictures she saw in her mind were far from what the audience was seeing on the large video screens on either side of the waterfall. In her mind, they were alone, in his music room, letting a warm spring breeze cool their heated bodies. The glass dome above them reminded her of the stars that must be shining as brightly as they had that night. She remembered the night as well as she remembered the song.

When his finger touched the last key, the crowd applauded nonstop. Amidst the din, Georgios turned to her, taking her hands. "I love you, Janeen. Nothing in my life matters more than having you by my side. I don't care about all this, I only care that I have you to share it with. Will you share it with me, Janeen? Will you become a part of my life?"

Janeen bit her lip. His handsome face became blurry as the moisture in her eyes spilled over. She'd wanted to tell him before, but couldn't because they'd had no privacy. Now she could tell him because the most private place in the world was there on that small bench between the two of them.

"Yes, Georgios. I love you."

He kissed her passionately to the sounds of cheers and whistles. The world was watching, but neither of them cared. The power of passion had brought them together.

KALEIDOSCOPE